NOT THIS WAY

(A Rachel Blackwood Suspense Thriller—Book One)

BLAKE PIERCE

Blake Pierce

Blake Pierce is the USA Today bestselling author of the RILEY PAGE mystery series, which includes seventeen books. Blake Pierce is also the author of the MACKENZIE WHITE mystery series, comprising fourteen books; of the AVERY BLACK mystery series, comprising six books; of the KERI LOCKE mystery series, comprising five books; of the MAKING OF RILEY PAIGE mystery series, comprising six books; of the KATE WISE mystery series, comprising seven books; of the CHLOE FINE psychological suspense mystery, comprising six books; of the JESSIE HUNT psychological suspense thriller series, comprising thirty-five books (and counting); of the AU PAIR psychological suspense thriller series, comprising three books; of the ZOE PRIME mystery series, comprising six books; of the ADELE SHARP mystery series, comprising sixteen books, of the EUROPEAN VOYAGE cozy mystery series, comprising six books; of the LAURA FROST FBI suspense thriller, comprising eleven books; of the ELLA DARK FBI suspense thriller, comprising twenty-one books (and counting); of the A YEAR IN EUROPE cozy mystery series, comprising nine books, of the AVA GOLD mystery series, comprising six books; of the RACHEL GIFT mystery series, comprising thirteen books (and counting); of the VALERIE LAW mystery series, comprising nine books; of the PAIGE KING mystery series, comprising eight books; of the MAY MOORE mystery series, comprising eleven books; of the CORA SHIELDS mystery series, comprising eight books; of the NICKY LYONS mystery series, comprising eight books, of the CAMI LARK mystery series, comprising ten books; of the AMBER YOUNG mystery series, comprising seven books (and counting); of the DAISY FORTUNE mystery series, comprising five books; of the FIONA RED mystery series, comprising eleven books (and counting); of the FAITH BOLD mystery series, comprising eleven books (and counting); of the JULIETTE HART mystery series, comprising five books (and counting); of the MORGAN CROSS mystery series, comprising nine books (and counting); of the FINN WRIGHT mystery series, comprising five books (and counting); of the new SHEILA STONE suspense thriller series, comprising five books (and counting); and of the new RACHEL BLACKWOOD suspense thriller series, comprising five books (and counting).

An avid reader and lifelong fan of the mystery and thriller genres, Blake loves to hear from you, so please feel free to visit www.blakepierceauthor.com to learn more and stay in touch.

ISBN: 978-1-0943-8355-2

BOOKS BY BLAKE PIERCE

RACHEL BLACKWOOD SUSPENSE THRILLER
NOT THIS WAY (Book #1)
NOT THIS TIME (Book #2)
NOT THIS CLOSE (Book #3)
NOT THIS ROAD (Book #4)
NOT THIS LATE (Book #5)

SHEILA STONE SUSPENSE THRILLER
SILENT GIRL (Book #1)
SILENT TRAIL (Book #2)
SILENT NIGHT (Book #3)
SILENT HOUSE (Book #4)
SILENT SCREAM (Book #5)

FINN WRIGHT MYSTERY SERIES
WHEN YOU'RE MINE (Book #1)
WHEN YOU'RE SAFE (Book #2)
WHEN YOU'RE CLOSE (Book #3)
WHEN YOU'RE SLEEPING (Book #4)
WHEN YOU'RE SANE (Book #5)

MORGAN CROSS MYSTERY SERIES
FOR YOU (Book #1)
FOR RAGE (Book #2)
FOR LUST (Book #3)
FOR WRATH (Book #4)
FOREVER (Book #5)
FOR US (Book #6)
FOR NOW (Book #7)
FOR ONCE (Book #8)
FOR ETERNITY (Book #9)

JULIETTE HART MYSTERY SERIES
NOTHING TO FEAR (Book #1)
NOTHING THERE (Book #2)
NOTHING WATCHING (Book #3)

NOTHING HIDING (Book #4)
NOTHING LEFT (Book #5)

FAITH BOLD MYSTERY SERIES
SO LONG (Book #1)
SO COLD (Book #2)
SO SCARED (Book #3)
SO NORMAL (Book #4)
SO FAR GONE (Book #5)
SO LOST (Book #6)
SO ALONE (Book #7)
SO FORGOTTEN (Book #8)
SO INSANE (Book #9)
SO SMITTEN (Book #10)
SO SIMPLE (Book #11)

FIONA RED MYSTERY SERIES
LET HER GO (Book #1)
LET HER BE (Book #2)
LET HER HOPE (Book #3)
LET HER WISH (Book #4)
LET HER LIVE (Book #5)
LET HER RUN (Book #6)
LET HER HIDE (Book #7)
LET HER BELIEVE (Book #8)
LET HER FORGET (Book #9)
LET HER TRY (Book #10)
LET HER PLAY (Book #11)

DAISY FORTUNE MYSTERY SERIES
NEED YOU (Book #1)
CLAIM YOU (Book #2)
CRAVE YOU (Book #3)
CHOOSE YOU (Book #4)
CHASE YOU (Book #5)

AMBER YOUNG MYSTERY SERIES
ABSENT PITY (Book #1)
ABSENT REMORSE (Book #2)
ABSENT FEELING (Book #3)
ABSENT MERCY (Book #4)

ABSENT REASON (Book #5)
ABSENT SANITY (Book #6)
ABSENT LIFE (Book #7)

CAMI LARK MYSTERY SERIES
JUST ME (Book #1)
JUST OUTSIDE (Book #2)
JUST RIGHT (Book #3)
JUST FORGET (Book #4)
JUST ONCE (Book #5)
JUST HIDE (Book #6)
JUST NOW (Book #7)
JUST HOPE (Book #8)
JUST LEAVE (Book #9)
JUST TONIGHT (Book #10)

NICKY LYONS MYSTERY SERIES
ALL MINE (Book #1)
ALL HIS (Book #2)
ALL HE SEES (Book #3)
ALL ALONE (Book #4)
ALL FOR ONE (Book #5)
ALL HE TAKES (Book #6)
ALL FOR ME (Book #7)
ALL IN (Book #8)

CORA SHIELDS MYSTERY SERIES
UNDONE (Book #1)
UNWANTED (Book #2)
UNHINGED (Book #3)
UNSAID (Book #4)
UNGLUED (Book #5)
UNSTABLE (Book #6)
UNKNOWN (Book #7)
UNAWARE (Book #8)

MAY MOORE SUSPENSE THRILLER
NEVER RUN (Book #1)
NEVER TELL (Book #2)
NEVER LIVE (Book #3)
NEVER HIDE (Book #4)

NEVER FORGIVE (Book #5)
NEVER AGAIN (Book #6)
NEVER LOOK BACK (Book #7)
NEVER FORGET (Book #8)
NEVER LET GO (Book #9)
NEVER PRETEND (Book #10)
NEVER HESITATE (Book #11)

PAIGE KING MYSTERY SERIES
THE GIRL HE PINED (Book #1)
THE GIRL HE CHOSE (Book #2)
THE GIRL HE TOOK (Book #3)
THE GIRL HE WISHED (Book #4)
THE GIRL HE CROWNED (Book #5)
THE GIRL HE WATCHED (Book #6)
THE GIRL HE WANTED (Book #7)
THE GIRL HE CLAIMED (Book #8)

VALERIE LAW MYSTERY SERIES
NO MERCY (Book #1)
NO PITY (Book #2)
NO FEAR (Book #3)
NO SLEEP (Book #4)
NO QUARTER (Book #5)
NO CHANCE (Book #6)
NO REFUGE (Book #7)
NO GRACE (Book #8)
NO ESCAPE (Book #9)

RACHEL GIFT MYSTERY SERIES
HER LAST WISH (Book #1)
HER LAST CHANCE (Book #2)
HER LAST HOPE (Book #3)
HER LAST FEAR (Book #4)
HER LAST CHOICE (Book #5)
HER LAST BREATH (Book #6)
HER LAST MISTAKE (Book #7)
HER LAST DESIRE (Book #8)
HER LAST REGRET (Book #9)
HER LAST HOUR (Book #10)
HER LAST SHOT (Book #11)

HER LAST PRAYER (Book #12)
HER LAST LIE (Book #13)

AVA GOLD MYSTERY SERIES
CITY OF PREY (Book #1)
CITY OF FEAR (Book #2)
CITY OF BONES (Book #3)
CITY OF GHOSTS (Book #4)
CITY OF DEATH (Book #5)
CITY OF VICE (Book #6)

A YEAR IN EUROPE
A MURDER IN PARIS (Book #1)
DEATH IN FLORENCE (Book #2)
VENGEANCE IN VIENNA (Book #3)
A FATALITY IN SPAIN (Book #4)

ELLA DARK FBI SUSPENSE THRILLER
GIRL, ALONE (Book #1)
GIRL, TAKEN (Book #2)
GIRL, HUNTED (Book #3)
GIRL, SILENCED (Book #4)
GIRL, VANISHED (Book 5)
GIRL ERASED (Book #6)
GIRL, FORSAKEN (Book #7)
GIRL, TRAPPED (Book #8)
GIRL, EXPENDABLE (Book #9)
GIRL, ESCAPED (Book #10)
GIRL, HIS (Book #11)
GIRL, LURED (Book #12)
GIRL, MISSING (Book #13)
GIRL, UNKNOWN (Book #14)
GIRL, DECEIVED (Book #15)
GIRL, FORLORN (Book #16)
GIRL, REMADE (Book #17)
GIRL, BETRAYED (Book #18)
GIRL, BOUND (Book #19)
GIRL, REFORMED (Book #20)
GIRL, REBORN (Book #21)

LAURA FROST FBI SUSPENSE THRILLER

ALREADY GONE (Book #1)
ALREADY SEEN (Book #2)
ALREADY TRAPPED (Book #3)
ALREADY MISSING (Book #4)
ALREADY DEAD (Book #5)
ALREADY TAKEN (Book #6)
ALREADY CHOSEN (Book #7)
ALREADY LOST (Book #8)
ALREADY HIS (Book #9)
ALREADY LURED (Book #10)
ALREADY COLD (Book #11)

EUROPEAN VOYAGE COZY MYSTERY SERIES
MURDER (AND BAKLAVA) (Book #1)
DEATH (AND APPLE STRUDEL) (Book #2)
CRIME (AND LAGER) (Book #3)
MISFORTUNE (AND GOUDA) (Book #4)
CALAMITY (AND A DANISH) (Book #5)
MAYHEM (AND HERRING) (Book #6)

ADELE SHARP MYSTERY SERIES
LEFT TO DIE (Book #1)
LEFT TO RUN (Book #2)
LEFT TO HIDE (Book #3)
LEFT TO KILL (Book #4)
LEFT TO MURDER (Book #5)
LEFT TO ENVY (Book #6)
LEFT TO LAPSE (Book #7)
LEFT TO VANISH (Book #8)
LEFT TO HUNT (Book #9)
LEFT TO FEAR (Book #10)
LEFT TO PREY (Book #11)
LEFT TO LURE (Book #12)
LEFT TO CRAVE (Book #13)
LEFT TO LOATHE (Book #14)
LEFT TO HARM (Book #15)
LEFT TO RUIN (Book #16)

THE AU PAIR SERIES
ALMOST GONE (Book#1)
ALMOST LOST (Book #2)

ALMOST DEAD (Book #3)

ZOE PRIME MYSTERY SERIES
FACE OF DEATH (Book#1)
FACE OF MURDER (Book #2)
FACE OF FEAR (Book #3)
FACE OF MADNESS (Book #4)
FACE OF FURY (Book #5)
FACE OF DARKNESS (Book #6)

A JESSIE HUNT PSYCHOLOGICAL SUSPENSE SERIES
THE PERFECT WIFE (Book #1)
THE PERFECT BLOCK (Book #2)
THE PERFECT HOUSE (Book #3)
THE PERFECT SMILE (Book #4)
THE PERFECT LIE (Book #5)
THE PERFECT LOOK (Book #6)
THE PERFECT AFFAIR (Book #7)
THE PERFECT ALIBI (Book #8)
THE PERFECT NEIGHBOR (Book #9)
THE PERFECT DISGUISE (Book #10)
THE PERFECT SECRET (Book #11)
THE PERFECT FAÇADE (Book #12)
THE PERFECT IMPRESSION (Book #13)
THE PERFECT DECEIT (Book #14)
THE PERFECT MISTRESS (Book #15)
THE PERFECT IMAGE (Book #16)
THE PERFECT VEIL (Book #17)
THE PERFECT INDISCRETION (Book #18)
THE PERFECT RUMOR (Book #19)
THE PERFECT COUPLE (Book #20)
THE PERFECT MURDER (Book #21)
THE PERFECT HUSBAND (Book #22)
THE PERFECT SCANDAL (Book #23)
THE PERFECT MASK (Book #24)
THE PERFECT RUSE (Book #25)
THE PERFECT VENEER (Book #26)
THE PERFECT PEOPLE (Book #27)
THE PERFECT WITNESS (Book #28)
THE PERFECT APPEARANCE (Book #29)
THE PERFECT TRAP (Book #30)

THE PERFECT EXPRESSION (Book #31)
THE PERFECT ACCOMPLICE (Book #32)
THE PERFECT SHOW (Book #33)
THE PERFECT POISE (Book #34)
THE PERFECT CROWD (Book #35)

CHLOE FINE PSYCHOLOGICAL SUSPENSE SERIES
NEXT DOOR (Book #1)
A NEIGHBOR'S LIE (Book #2)
CUL DE SAC (Book #3)
SILENT NEIGHBOR (Book #4)
HOMECOMING (Book #5)
TINTED WINDOWS (Book #6)

KATE WISE MYSTERY SERIES
IF SHE KNEW (Book #1)
IF SHE SAW (Book #2)
IF SHE RAN (Book #3)
IF SHE HID (Book #4)
IF SHE FLED (Book #5)
IF SHE FEARED (Book #6)
IF SHE HEARD (Book #7)

THE MAKING OF RILEY PAIGE SERIES
WATCHING (Book #1)
WAITING (Book #2)
LURING (Book #3)
TAKING (Book #4)
STALKING (Book #5)
KILLING (Book #6)

RILEY PAIGE MYSTERY SERIES
ONCE GONE (Book #1)
ONCE TAKEN (Book #2)
ONCE CRAVED (Book #3)
ONCE LURED (Book #4)
ONCE HUNTED (Book #5)
ONCE PINED (Book #6)
ONCE FORSAKEN (Book #7)
ONCE COLD (Book #8)
ONCE STALKED (Book #9)

ONCE LOST (Book #10)
ONCE BURIED (Book #11)
ONCE BOUND (Book #12)
ONCE TRAPPED (Book #13)
ONCE DORMANT (Book #14)
ONCE SHUNNED (Book #15)
ONCE MISSED (Book #16)
ONCE CHOSEN (Book #17)

MACKENZIE WHITE MYSTERY SERIES
BEFORE HE KILLS (Book #1)
BEFORE HE SEES (Book #2)
BEFORE HE COVETS (Book #3)
BEFORE HE TAKES (Book #4)
BEFORE HE NEEDS (Book #5)
BEFORE HE FEELS (Book #6)
BEFORE HE SINS (Book #7)
BEFORE HE HUNTS (Book #8)
BEFORE HE PREYS (Book #9)
BEFORE HE LONGS (Book #10)
BEFORE HE LAPSES (Book #11)
BEFORE HE ENVIES (Book #12)
BEFORE HE STALKS (Book #13)
BEFORE HE HARMS (Book #14)

AVERY BLACK MYSTERY SERIES
CAUSE TO KILL (Book #1)
CAUSE TO RUN (Book #2)
CAUSE TO HIDE (Book #3)
CAUSE TO FEAR (Book #4)
CAUSE TO SAVE (Book #5)
CAUSE TO DREAD (Book #6)

KERI LOCKE MYSTERY SERIES
A TRACE OF DEATH (Book #1)
A TRACE OF MURDER (Book #2)
A TRACE OF VICE (Book #3)
A TRACE OF CRIME (Book #4)
A TRACE OF HOPE (Book #5)

PROLOGUE

The blare of the alarm jolted Candace awake. She blinked rapidly, trying to orient herself in the cramped sleeping cubicle. Her first day on the rig. This was it.

She threw on her coveralls and work boots, stumbling into the hallway. The stale air reeked of oil and sweat. Machinery hummed and clanked, the steel walkways vibrating under her feet as she made her way topside.

Candace emerged onto the platform and stiffened, feeling a low, nervous energy under the rising light of dawn. Massive drills and cranes towered above her, drenched in glaring floodlights. The rig looked like an oil-slicked metal beast come to life. Veterans strode past with clenched jaws, ignoring the newbie gawking in their midst.

Over the deafening grind of the drills, the foreman shouted orders. Candace tried to focus amidst the sensory assault—the acidic tang of crude oil, the searing wind whipping her hair. She was here to do a job, to prove herself.

As she headed toward her station, Candace steeled her nerves and whispered, "You got this."

She joined the other workers at the control station, trying to make sense of the panel's blinking lights and gauges.

"Rookie, check the pressure in valve 6C," grunted Hank, the grizzled driller.

Candace fumbled with the controls. The readings seemed off.

"Trouble?" asked Hank.

"Pressure's dropping fast in 6C," Candace replied.

Hank scowled. "Equipment's acting up again. We better shut it down before she blows."

He killed the power on the drill, bringing an eerie silence to the platform. The crew gathered around as Hank examined the malfunctioning valve, his brow furrowed.

"This thing's busted good," he muttered. "Gonna take some time to fix. Whole operation's stalled 'til then."

The workers grumbled but got to work stopping the flow of oil and gas. As the floodlights illuminated their efforts, she wondered if this was what every shift out here was like—wrestling with temperamental machines to keep the crude pumping.

"Alright, let's troubleshoot this mess," Hank muttered at her side. "Smith, check the intake lines. Johnson, inspect the seals. Rookie, monitor the sensors and let me know if you see any spikes."

The workers dispersed to their tasks. Candace kept her eyes glued to the sensor panel. The readings seemed steady. Then, without warning, the pressure spiked in valve 6C. Lights flashed as the sensors went haywire.

"Hank! We've got a problem over here!" Candace yelled.

Hank rushed over. "What the hell? Valve's jumping all over the place."

The crew gathered around the panel, faces etched with concern. The rig creaked and groaned as pressure built.

"Shut it down, now!" Hank barked.

Candace scrambled to power down the valve before it ruptured. The noise died away as the sensors stabilized.

Hank let out a low whistle. "This thing's possessed. Almost lost control there. We gotta find the root of the problem before the whole rig's compromised."

Candace nodded, heart pounding. She wasn't expecting her first day to involve averting a blowout. Maybe she had gotten in over her head. But it was too late to turn back now.

The crew fanned out across the platform, searching for clues. Candace followed Hank as he inspected the pipes and valves leading from the troublesome valve. She kept one eye on the sensor panel, ready to alert them if readings spiked again.

Hank scratched his head as they circled back around. "Can't find a damn thing wrong. But something's making that valve go haywire."

He gazed across the rig, pondering their next move. His eyes landed on an access port along the outer railing.

"There," he said, pointing. "Service hatch. Leads right to the valve junction. We get eyes down there, maybe we can spot the culprit."

Candace and Hank made their way to the port. Hank wheeled over a work light and flipped the switch, illuminating the dark hole. Candace peered down into the abyss, a chill running through her. This was no place for claustrophobes.

Hank lowered himself partway into the hole. "Hand me that flashlight, will ya?"

Candace passed him a heavy-duty flashlight. Hank's upper body disappeared as he angled the light beam down the narrow passage.

"See anything?" Candace asked, a knot in her stomach. If they couldn't find the problem here, she wasn't sure where else to look.

Hank didn't respond right away. He shifted, craning his neck to see deeper into the hole. Candace held her breath.

After an agonizing moment, Hank hauled himself back up. "Shit," he muttered under his breath, rubbing at his flank.

"What?" she said.

"Too fat," he muttered, providing a chuckle. He winked at her. "Looks like you gotta go down there, rook."

She stared at him.

"I ain't joking. Come on now. We pay you the big bucks for this."

Candace didn't think they were paying her *that* big of bucks.

Still, she couldn't look like a coward on the first day of the job.

And so, summoning her nerve, she nodded, accepting a headlamp from Hank and slipping past him as he pulled his girth from the hatch.

Then, with a deep swallow, peering into the dark and trying to hide the way her hands trembled against the ladder, she descended into the murk.

Candace dropped into the claustrophobic darkness with a single goal in mind: find the problem and fix it. She clung tightly to the ladder rungs, her headlamp illuminating the narrow walls of the passage. The air was thick with the smell of oil and metal.

The passage seemed to go on forever, twisting and turning at odd angles. Candace's heart pounded in her chest as she imagined getting stuck down here, trapped in the dark. She shook her head, banishing the thought. She had a job to do.

At last, the passage opened up into a small chamber. Candace shone her headlamp around, and there, in the dark, against a stone wall, she spotted something.

She hesitated, staring, a frown creasing her features.

She took a couple of shuffling steps forward.

"See anything?" Hank's voice called from above.

She didn't reply. Didn't want to open her mouth and swallow the fumes.

Candace steeled herself and leaned over, peering past a rail into an opening in the ground.

She clicked on the flashlight's second, brighter setting and directed the beam down into the shadows.

There, about twenty feet down, a pale shape lay crumpled on the metal floor. As her eyes adjusted, details emerged from the gloom. A ruffled dress soaked with dark fluids. Lank hair obscuring the face. Arms and legs splayed at unnatural angles.

Candace recoiled, bile rising in her throat.

"See anything?" Hank called again.

Candace held back the tremor in her voice. She yelled up the hatch, "Call the cops! We have a corpse."

CHAPTER ONE

The thicket snapped behind Rachel Blackwood as she plunged into the forest, her boots sinking into the spongy earth with every stride.

On the mossy branch of a toppled tree, her white Stetson sat on a folded leather jacket. A girl had to protect her hat.

Her night-black hair caressed her features as she sprinted. The small aquamarine beads woven into her fringe tapped against her ear as she ran, a constant, rhythmic reminder of the pounding in her chest.

Her feet were surefooted on the rough terrain, thanks to decades of tracking, sprinting through rough terrain, and navigating the wilderness and forgotten places of Texas.

And the area near Caddo Lake was no exception. A hauntingly beautiful backdrop with its swamps, Spanish moss–draped trees, and waterways.

Spanish moss caressed her face like spectral fingers as she ducked under gnarled branches.

Her heart pounded in time with her footsteps, fueled by anticipation and rage. After three months of dead ends, she had him. The killer who had butchered three Native women. This time, it was personal.

She gritted her teeth against the memories threatening to surface and poured on more speed. The dense woods of Caddo Lake were her home terrain. She knew every root, every hollow, every creature that slithered through its depths.

He didn’t stand a chance.

A snap of a twig. The rustle of leaves. There, ahead, a flicker of movement. Her rifle was in her hands in an instant, the scope finding its target. A dark figure crouched behind a cypress tree, chest heaving.

Stefan Camden. Wall Street boy having returned to his roots in Texas.

A psychopath, through and through.

Judging by what he’d done to those women, he’d really enjoyed the pain he inflicted.

She stared through her scope at the crouched figure.

As a Texas Ranger, and a big-game hunter in a past life, she’d sat on this side of a scope countless times before, eyeing a predator.

She frowned, her finger steady on the trigger, but her discipline took over.

Her path to becoming a Ranger in the great state hadn't been a linear one.

She had started as a wildlife biologist, studying the habits of the animals she now hunted. She didn't hunt to kill, but to protect. Big game, like mountain lions, would rip small herds of sheep apart. Ruining livelihoods, tearing through entire herds… Sometimes, though a painful truth, a well-placed bullet spared many lives.

And other times, she went after bigger game.

That was how she had ended up here, in the heart of the forest, ready to bring Stefan Camden to justice.

She watched him for a few more moments, observing his every movement. He seemed to be muttering to himself, his eyes darting around, searching for an escape route. Rachel had him cornered, and he knew it.

Got you.

She moved closer, as silent as the shadows, senses primed. He didn't hear her.

Didn't hear a single sound. She could move like that, in the dark, creeping forward without anyone noticing her. For decades—almost three, to be precise—she'd spent her life moving in the woods.

Camden was waiting in ambush, she realized.

She could've shot him.

Could've attacked him from behind.

But where was the fair play in that?

Even predators had the right to a fair fight. He lay in ambush? So be it. Let him. She welcomed it.

So she took a step intentionally on a fallen, dried branch.

Crack.

He whirled around. Eyes widened in his panicked, blond features. When he sprang with a roar, knife glinting, she was ready.

They crashed to the ground, a tangle of limbs. She landed a punch, felt the satisfying crunch of bone. He slashed wildly with his knife, scoring a line of fire across her arm. She barely felt it.

Grappling had also been part of her training. Not a family tradition. She'd never been able to spend much time with her father, after all. Nor her mother. Growing up an orphan, one had to pick up skills from various sources.

So her aunt, the woman who'd raised her, had been the expert.

And now, Rachel maneuvered with quick, meticulous precision.

By alerting him to her presence, she'd given him a fair shot. But that was all the dignity he'd get. He hadn't trained a day in his life—she could feel it in his tense frame, his panicked breathing. His slick, damp clothing.

The fight wasn't even that. Within seconds, she'd disarmed him, using his own shoulder to press the flat of the blade into the mud.

And then she transitioned from a triangle choke into an armbar.

With a swift move, she pinned him face-down in the mud, wrenching his arm behind his back. "You're under arrest," she growled. He was gasping. She wasn't even breathing heavily. She hauled him to his feet.

He cursed at her, trying to scratch her or stamp at her foot.

She caught his ankle, hooking it with her heel and tripping him. He hit the mud again.

He tried to rise, but she shoved him down again, and his breath escaped in a puff.
"Stop," she said simply.

He snarled, trying to go for his knife.

And so her six-shooter appeared in one hand. Another gift from her aunt. She pointed the weapon at his head. Only six bullets, compared to some pistols now used. She didn't have twelve shots, or twenty. So the ones she did have had to matter more.

Her aim was as deadly as her tracking skills.

"I said stop," she said in a firm voice.

He stared up at her, blinking, staring down the barrel of the gun.

She hauled him to his feet, cuffing his hands behind his back.

"How'd you find me?" he said, glaring at her.

She didn't reply. He'd tried to trick them. Had cast his scent in different directions with an old shirt, a sweater. He'd gone through mud and soaked his shirt in doe urine. She could smell it on him.

But it hadn't mattered. She wasn't a bloodhound. Scent didn't matter nearly as much as the whispers of the forest. Cracked branches, ruffled leaves, disheveled detritus.

And something more. A bone-deep connection to this land, to its whispers and warnings. A legacy from her Native American heritage, from the aunt who'd raised her and taught her to track and hunt.

The killer spat at her feet. "You think you've won?" he sneered.

Suddenly, there was a burst of motion from behind her.

She glanced back.

Feds. FBI.

Sometimes they played ball with the Rangers.

But they were clumsy in the dark. Still, she kept her expression polite. She'd learned long ago that not everyone could move in the woods like she and her aunt could.

Now, six feds emerged from the woods, cursing and slapping at bugs. One nearly tripped into a stream.

The man in the lead—a squat fellow shaped like a pit bull with jowls to match—reached her first. Nodded in greeting. He had a confident swagger about him. His muscles had muscles.

She nodded back. "Agent Santino."

"Nice collar."

"Thanks." She shrugged. "You got it from here?"

He looked at her, surprised. Usually, feds liked to get credit for their collars. But Rachel had never really understood the allure of a fast-tracked career.

Office work?

She'd rather swallow glass.

Agent Santino accepted Camden, who was still cursing, uttering racial epithets at this point.

The feds seemed all too grateful to retreat from the woods. She received a couple of nods of gratitude, but mostly, the feds just hurried off, carrying their suspect with them.

Rachel watched the killer disappear into the dense forest, her keen eyes tracking his movement. The other agents rushed past, distracted by a splash in the murky waters.

She tried not to smile. An alligator was watching them from a stream bed, but none of them had spotted it.

Her pulse quickened as she moved silently through the underbrush, guided by instincts honed since childhood. Broken twigs, displaced leaves, the faint snap of a branch all formed a trail only she could follow.

A far more important trail to her.

One that led back to her white hat with the single eagle feather tucked in the brim.

She was no longer aware of the damp earth beneath her boots or the mosquitoes buzzing about her face.

There. A glimpse of faded white between the trees. She adjusted her course, keeping downwind so nothing ahead might catch her scent.

She approached her hat. Snatched it off her folded leather jacket. The hat settled on her head, fitting snug like a hug.

She smiled.

Her phone was sitting in the pocket of her leather jacket. She wrinkled her nose. She and technology got along like water and oil.

But as she stared at the jacket, she noticed the pocket glowing.

A second later, her phone began to chirp.

Normally, she kept the phone on silent, but only one number caused the device to ring.

Work.

She picked up the phone. "Yes?"

"Blackwood, that you?"

"Mhmm."

"You done with that side quest for the feds? We got something."

She blinked. So soon? Normally, it was rare to boomerang a Ranger. Assigning them from one high-priority case quickly to another. But she didn't protest. Instead, she said, "Now?"

"Yeah. Right now. This shit's gonna hit the fan soon. News agencies. Online bloggers. That sorta shit. You comin'?"

"Yeah. On my way."

She adjusted her hat, snatched her scoped rifle, and hurried off through the woods, back toward where she'd parked her rusted-out Jeep.

CHAPTER TWO

Back at the Texas Department of Public Safety, the lobby's fluorescent lights glared down as Rachel pushed through the glass doors.

Out of the corner of her eye, she spotted Camden in cuffs being led by a couple of feds toward booking. His greasy hair hung limply across his forehead, but his dark eyes were alert, scanning the room until they settled on Rachel. His thin lips curled into a leer.

She didn't look away.

He'd killed three Native women. He might've killed her in another life.

She didn't believe with all her training, all of her skills, that she was immune to a bullet or a blade.

One had to be practical about such things.

As she stood in the lobby, she caught a thumbs-up flashed in her direction from the receptionist. Gabriel Ingles winked at her, his round, smiling face beaming.

"Nice one, Blackwood!" he called.

She nodded back at him, her solemn features serious as ever.

"Oh come on, can't spare a smile?" Gabriel called out. He wiggled his eyebrows. "I hear you beat those feds to the mark by nearly half an hour. Good. Fuck 'em."

She allowed a smile to curve her lips and winked at Gabriel. He basked in the glow of her smile—it was a rare thing for Rachel to smile, and when she allowed one across her features, it was like an offered gift to anyone who spotted it.

Before Rachel could spiral further into *too* much good humor, a strong hand gripped her shoulder. A *very* strong hand, like the steel cords on some giant ship. She turned to see Thomas Greywolf, his weathered face creased in a frown.

He eyed her up and down like a master woodworker examining a live edge plank.

"I'm fine," she said.

"Your arm." He nodded at where he'd spotted a thin trickle of blood seeping through her sleeve.

"Just a scratch."

"Did you get it checked?"

"Just a scratch, Thomas," she said.

He sighed heavily, his weathered features serving as a fixture for his rolling eyes. As his eyeballs circumnavigated their sockets, he let out an exasperated sigh.

"You really need to take better care of yourself, little jackdaw."

She smirked at the nickname and patted the brawny, middle-aged Native man on his arm.

Thomas was the only other Native at the Ranger headquarters in her department. He'd taken her under his wing years ago, when she'd first joined, and had a soft spot for her.

Secretly, she assumed this was because Thomas and his wife often took in orphans. They'd adopted five kids over the years. He had a tender heart toward people who grew up like he had, without parents.

The two of them had bonded instantly.

Now, he was giving her a fatherly look—equal parts exasperation and pride.

"Is it true you took him yourself?"

"Mhmm."

"The feds were slow in the forest?"

She grinned. "What do you think?"

He grinned back, his features wrinkling once more. Unlike Rachel's, Thomas's smile was an ever-present, ever-reliable occurrence, like a sunrise.

Thomas glanced around the room, then gently steered her toward a quiet corner. His eyes were kind but solemn.

"You did good today," he said. "Real good."

She hesitated though, watching him closely. Something in his tone immediately put her on guard. "But…" she said, quirking an eyebrow.

"But," he replied softly, "Captain Smith is furious you went in without backup. I know you felt you had no choice…" Thomas held up a hand as Rachel opened her mouth to protest. "I know. Just…watch your back with him. The Captain won't forget this."

Rachel exhaled, her shoulders slumping. Standing under the bright fluorescent bulbs, she felt out of place. She missed the woods, the scent of moss and petrichor. She missed camping in the rain, listening to the drizzle and the scamper of creatures.

And now… Captain Smith. He had always had it out for her. Even if she'd done *everything* by the book and had waited for the feds to show up on time, he likely still would've found something to be annoyed with.

"I can take care of myself," Rachel said quietly. It wasn't a prideful claim, just a practical reminder. She tilted the brim of her hat, the eagle feather fluttering in the air from the ceiling AC unit.

Thomas nodded. "I know you can. But even warriors need allies sometimes." He gave her shoulder a final squeeze. "Just remember you've got me in your corner."

Rachel managed a real smile then.

She had barely stepped away from Thomas when a booming voice cut through the din of the lobby.

"Blackwood! My office. Now."

Captain Smith stood in the doorway of his office, face like thunder. He had a thin chin-strap and a neat, pressed blue suit that proudly displayed a golden skeleton watch on his right wrist. The chatter in the lobby from near the desk died instantly as all eyes turned to Rachel. She lifted her chin, ignoring the darting glances and hushed murmurs, and walked steadily across the room.

Each click of her shoes on the tile echoed the rapid beat of her heart. She schooled her features into a neutral mask, determined not to show weakness. Not to Captain Smith.

The Captain's cold eyes tracked her approach. When she drew close, he ran a hand through his gelled hair, spun on his heel, and stalked into his office without a word. The door snapped shut behind him.

Rachel paused, steadying herself with a slow breath, as if she were about to aim through a scope.

Squaring her shoulders, as if against a blustering mountain wind, Rachel turned the knob and stepped inside to meet her fate.

Captain Smith stood with his back to the door, arms crossed as he gazed out the window overlooking the city. Rachel hovered just inside the room, unsure if she should speak first.

After a tense moment, the Captain broke the silence without turning around. "That was a damn foolish thing you did today, Blackwood. Going in alone like that."

His gravelly voice was cold, clipped. Rachel bristled but bit back a sharp retort.

"With all due respect, sir, he would've escaped if I'd waited—"

Smith whirled on her, eyes flashing. "I don't give a damn about your excuses!" He advanced until he towered over her, using his height to intimidate. "You deliberately disobeyed a direct order and put yourself and others at risk with that little stunt."

He smelled of copious amounts of cologne. She didn't mention it.

Rachel stood her ground. When a grizzly approached, one didn't want to show weakness. She also didn't say a word. The Captain seemed in a lecturing mode; she would hold her tongue until he gave her reason to loosen it.

The Captain's face turned an alarming shade of purple at her stoic silence. He was shaking his head now, a single strand of gelled hair falling from his hirsute helmet of product and dye. For a moment, Rachel thought he might actually strike her. But he mastered himself with visible effort, stepping back and resuming his stern pose.

"You're damn lucky the operation succeeded, Blackwood," he bit out. "If we're going to make any progress on repairing relations with the tribal council, I can't have my agents going off half-cocked on their own agendas and private land."

He pinned her with an icy stare. "Consider this your last warning. I've got my eye on you now. One more misstep, and you're off this task force for good."

Rachel hesitated, but kept her expression neutral. He'd given her this speech more than once. As of yet, she hadn't been booted. She still wasn't exactly sure why he disliked her, though she had some guesses. "Is that all, sir?"

Smith gave a curt nod. "For now. But don't get too comfortable. I've got another case for you—a big one. It's going to be splashed all over the papers." His eyes glinted. "Think you can handle that…or should I find someone else?"

The challenge in his voice was unmistakable. Rachel met his gaze steadily. "I can handle it, sir." She hesitated briefly, wondering if he wanted to yell at her a bit more.

But he had turned to his desk now and was wearily massaging the bridge of his nose, shaking his head as he did.

"Do you know who Madison Beaumont is?"

"I don't."

He blinked. "Really? Her family's in the papers a lot."

"I don't read the news," she said simply.

Again, she received a disbelieving look. But Captain Smith, as he often did, had bounced from one emotion to the next.

Now his rage was gone, and his frustration had returned. But the frustration, at least in part, seemed directed to the file open on his computer. He drummed his fingers against the keyboard in thought as he said, "Heiress to the Austin Drilling outfit."

This, Rachel *had* heard of. More than one dispute with her people had occurred over drilling rights on reservation land.

"The oil company?"

"That's the one. A multibillion-dollar oil company."

She blinked. "And Ms. Beaumont is dead?"

"Yeah. Found this morning on a drill site. Got some of the locals spooked. We're keeping a lid on it for now. But a billionaire found dead in her own oil field? That's gonna make some headlines. Think you can keep your face out of the press?"

She wasn't sure what he was implying by this. But again, as Thomas had often told her, don't let them *bait* you.

So she kept her expression stoic. She nodded once. "Yes, sir."

"Alright. Then what the hell are you still standing around here for? Get going, Blackwood." He flashed her a final frown, then returned to the computer.

She nodded once, then moved swiftly to the door. Her arm didn't bother her, though she could feel needles of pain. She hadn't been tired by her run through the woods, nor her scuffle with Camden.

The ten minutes back at HQ?

Downright exhausting.

But another high-profile case? Just the thing to get the blood pumping. She strode purposefully out of the office, moving with precision toward the sliding glass doors.

A billionaire tycoon found dead on an oil field that had run-ins with Natives.

She wondered if *that* was why Smith had assigned her. Hoping to find cause to fire her, perhaps hoping trouble would arise because of her roots.

But as a half-Native woman, she'd learned to navigate the politics of the Rangers.

And now, all she wanted was to start the hunt.

CHAPTER THREE

The watchful man's eyes narrowed as he stared out through the windshield, his knuckles white from gripping the steering wheel. The small wooden charm dangling from his mirror clacked against the glass as it rattled on beads. His breathing was steady despite the adrenaline coursing through his veins. This was it. This was the moment he had been waiting for.

He glanced down at the photo of his next victim taped to the dashboard. Young. Naive. Vulnerable. An easy target. The perfect sacrifice for his ritual.

"Don't worry, my dear, it will all be over soon," he muttered under his breath, his voice a chilling whisper.

The car glided silently down the street as he tracked his prey. Up ahead, a young woman walked alone, her pace brisk. She had no idea what was coming. No idea that these were her final moments of freedom.

Closer and closer he crept, anticipation rising. His heart pounded against his ribs like a caged animal, hungry for what would come next. The world narrowed down to just the two of them now. Predator and prey. Killer and victim. This was his design.

When she turned down the empty alley, he seized his chance. The car leaped forward, engine growling as he raced to cut off her escape. She glanced back, eyes wide with sudden terror as she realized too late that she had made a fatal mistake.

He was upon her.

The woman stared in fear as the car screeched to a halt, blocking her only exit. She turned to run, but it was already too late.

The killer threw open the door, moving swiftly to cut off her escape. She let out a panicked scream as he grabbed her, clamping a gloved hand over her mouth.

"Shhh…it will all be over soon," he whispered. She struggled violently, terror etched on her face.

He dragged her toward the open trunk as she kicked and flailed. But he was too strong. Her muffled cries became more frantic as he forced her inside the cramped space.

She clawed at him, but he did not react. His face was a cold, emotionless mask. This was all part of the ritual.

He bound her wrists, grabbing duct tape. Securing her, holding her fast. She was so weak under his efforts.

He slammed the trunk closed, enveloping her in darkness. Her screams were silenced, replaced by the thud of fists pounding against the inside of the trunk. He slid back into the driver's seat, exhilarated.

Soon, the earth would feed. The corruptors would pay, and he would fade back into the shadows, leaving the police baffled once again.

For now, all that remained was the long drive. His passenger continued to pound the trunk.

The watchful man drove steadily into the night, following the remote dirt roads that wound through the dense forest. His destination was an abandoned oil field, hidden deep in the wilderness where no one ventured anymore.

He smiled to himself, anticipation building. This was his favorite part—the hunt, the capture, and now the final ceremony. His pulse quickened at the thought of what was to come. What he lovingly referred to as "the feeding."

Glancing in the rearview mirror, he could just make out the trunk of the vintage Plymouth. His cargo was secure. The girl had given up fighting, no doubt conserving her energy. She would need it later, when her screams echoed through the empty night.

For now, the drive was peaceful. His headlights cut a lonely path through the darkness. The moon above gave the forest an ethereal glow. An owl hooted, unseen, in the blackness.

The girl in the trunk was probably praying now, pleading for her life.

The killer continued onward through the night. His senses were alive, electric. The anticipation was almost unbearable now.

The abandoned oil field waited, hidden in the shadows. The girl, his sacrificial lamb, unknowing.

He slowed the car as it approached the old access road leading to the oil field. He had driven this remote path many times before, the way carved into his memory. The Plymouth's worn tires crunched over gravel and dirt, a lonely sound swallowed by the vast emptiness.

Up ahead, the skeletal outlines of abandoned rigs rose from the darkness. They stood as silent sentinels, witnesses to what was about to transpire. He felt a reverence in their presence, a link to past rituals carried out in this unholy place.

As the car rolled to a stop, the world seemed to hold its breath. Even the night creatures stilled, as if in deference to sacred ceremonies older than man. He stepped out, inhaling the cool air. Above him, the stars glittered coldly.

Popping the trunk, he looked down at his prize. The girl lay curled on her side, wrists and ankles bound. A strip of duct tape silenced her pleas. As she looked up at him with wide, terrified eyes, he felt a heady rush of power.

"Welcome," he whispered.

Reaching down, he hauled her roughly to her feet. She stumbled, weak from the disorienting ride. Holding her firm, he led her toward the oil pit.

The girl twisted in his grip, whimpering against the gag. He slapped her hard, the crack echoing between the lifeless rigs.

"Hush now," he crooned. "No one can hear you."

As he dragged her onward, his boots crunched over something brittle. Glancing down, he saw a smattering of twigs—old offerings left to bleach beneath the pitiless sun. They snapped under his steps, reduced to shards.

He pulled a hunting knife from his belt.

The girl stared and nearly fainted, but he merely cut the girl's bonds.

The girl's chest heaved, eyes tracking the knife. He imagined the frenzied hammering of her heart, a trapped bird throwing itself against her ribs.

"Shhh," he murmured, tracing the blade down her cheek. "Your blood will nourish this forgotten land. You should feel honored."

She squeezed her eyes shut, tears sliding down her face. He smiled. It was time.

"Now run," he said simply. "You have a chance to run. It's the test. The final one. If you outpace me, I'll let you live."

She stared at him.

He smiled. "They never outpace me. Now *run*!"

She screamed, breaking into a sprint, racing in the opposite direction.

He watched her flee, enjoying the sight.

And then he broke into a canter of his own until the night swallowed them both.

CHAPTER FOUR

Rachel stepped outside the Austin headquarters, her boots crunching on the gravel. A black sedan idled near the entrance, exhaust curling from its tailpipe into the crisp morning air.

Must be her new partner. She sighed, walking over and peering into the driver's side window. A man glanced up, startled. "Ranger Blackwood?"

"That's me."

He scrambled out of the car, hand extended. "Ethan Morgan. Homicide PD, newly transferred. I guess that makes me a Ranger now." He beamed at her.

Rachel shook his hand once, releasing it quickly. She knew his name and rank, nothing more. The brass shuffled partners often, but she preferred working alone. Few could keep up—quite literally. She was fleet-footed.

Ethan opened the passenger door. Rachel slid inside, leather creaking, and stared out the window as he settled into the driver's seat.

"So, uh, you've been a Ranger how long?" Ethan asked, voice tentative.

Rachel kept her response curt. "Five years."

"Impressive." A pause. "This your first big case?"

Her jaw tightened. She said nothing. No need to scare him on his first day.

Ethan's Adam's apple bobbed as he swallowed hard, shifting into gear.

The sedan rolled forward, buildings blurring outside Rachel's window. Her fingers curled into fists on her thighs. She had a job to do, and personal feelings didn't factor into it. But Captain Smith had gone out of his way to browbeat her.

Likely, he wanted—*expected*—her to fail.

But she'd faced worse before.

Still, she couldn't ignore the twinge in her gut. The heiress's murder would attract publicity, and she despised politics. But if it led to the truth, she'd weather the storm.

Ethan was speaking again, and she picked up on his thick, southern drawl now. The more comfortable he got, the more it came out.

She glanced at him. He had freckles and close-cut, military hair. His jaw and cheekbones were pronounced, suggesting a very low body-fat percentage.

Her eyes slipped down his tight, button-up flannel, and she wondered if the rest of him matched.

Ethan's dark brown hair was trimmed neatly but with a slight hint of ruggedness and the occasional cowlick lending him an endearing touch of boyishness.

He noticed her attention and glanced over with a wink. "Like what you see?"

Instantly, he seemed to realize this wasn't proper for fellow coworkers meeting for the first time.

"Shit, sorry. I'm nervous. I joke when I'm nervous." He grimaced in her direction.

She didn't comment. She'd been considering the size of his abdominal muscles, so she decided they were even.

As they left the city, Rachel stared out the window as scrubby fields whipped by, broken only by ramshackle barns and livestock. The familiar sight usually calmed her, but today it only amplified her tension.

Beside her, Ethan cleared his throat again. "So, uh, what can you tell me about the case?"

She kept her response concise. "Wealthy heiress, drowned in oil. Body found by a neophyte oil worker."

"No signs of a struggle, though, right?" Ethan glanced at her. "Had to be someone she knew."

Rachel's jaw tightened. She wouldn't speculate, not this early. "We'll see what the evidence shows."

Ethan shrugged again but didn't push further.

Scrub gave way to sun-scorched grass as they turned onto the private road leading to the Beaumont ranch, one of the largest in Texas. Rachel leaned forward, the knot in her gut tightening.

The ranch spread before them, barbed wire fencing stretching to the horizon. A sprawling hacienda rose in the distance, Spanish-style architecture weathered by time and the elements.

Rachel studied the house, a frown making its way into her features. Something about its isolation bothered her, though she couldn't pinpoint why.

Ethan pulled up beside a line of patrol cars and cut the engine. "Here we are."

Here they were. Rachel exhaled slowly, steeling herself, and pushed open the sedan door. The Texas sun beat down as she made her way toward the hacienda, a looming silhouette against the cloudless sky.

Rachel approached the front entrance, ducking under the yellow crime scene tape. The heavy oak door creaked open.

Cool darkness enveloped her as she stepped inside. The foyer stretched before them, tiled floors and arched entryways leading to other wings of the house.

"So… they found the body here?" Ethan asked at her side.

She shook her head.

"You're not very talkative, are you?"

"Not really," she said. Then, deciding he deserved a bit more, she said, "Madison Beaumont lived alone in the house. They're using this as a temporary staging area until the coroner gets here."

"Oh. Huh." He scratched at a cowlick, trying to smooth his hair, but the stubborn curl bounced right back up. In a way, it made her think of the man himself.

Determinedly good-humored, it seemed. He was still wearing that easy smile.

She pointed toward the white tarp on the ground which had prompted the question.

The body had been brought to the ranch. Due to the heat outside, and the air-conditioning in the ranch, the body had been placed in the main foyer.

In the center of the ornately tiled floor, the body lay draped in a white sheet, a pool of black ink seeping across the tiles. Oil from the corpse.

Rachel's jaw tightened. No matter how many crime scenes she processed, death never got easier to face.

Ethan hesitated beside her, eyes lingering on the shrouded form. "Guess we found our victim." His attempt at humor fell flat.

Rachel said nothing as she walked forward, kneeling beside the body. With a gloved hand, she folded back the sheet to reveal the victim's face.

Pale, lifeless skin. Glassy, unseeing eyes. Oil-stained flesh visible in the ruin of the woman's temple.

Rachel straightened, scanning the foyer. No signs of a break-in or struggle.

"She wasn't at work that early," Rachel said, straightening. She frowned, trying to recall the case file she'd read on the walk to the car outside HQ. "She sleeps alone here, but has security."

At these words, Ethan glanced up. He pointed. "Eye in the sky."

Rachel followed his gaze, impressed. Her new partner had a quick eye, apparently. He'd spotted the camera above quite quickly.

Rachel studied the foyer, taking in details with a practiced eye. Polished marble floors. Vaulted ceilings. An ostentatious chandelier dripping with crystals.

Wealth and power on display. The perfect setting for a political execution.

"No signs of a break-in," Ethan said. "She must have let the killer in herself."

"If this really was the location of the abduction."

"You don't think some rich lady yuckity-yuck was out strolling the oil fields, do you?"

"I don't know yet."

She crossed the foyer, pushing open the doors to reveal a spacious room lined with bookshelves. A heavy oak desk. Leather armchairs arranged before a fireplace, cold and dark.

"What is it?" Ethan asked at her side.

"Door was shut."

"So?"

"None of the other doors are shut."

"What does that mean?"

Rachel shrugged. Not everything had to *mean* something. Sometimes, a tracker's best bet was just to spot what was unlike the other things. What was out of place.

She glanced at a large window in the back. Latched.

She frowned, moving around the table, her eyes combing the carpet. Books disheveled.

"Wait a second."

"What?" Ethan said.

"The books."

"I mean… I've read before, just not those."

"No, I wasn't asking if you've read them. They're out of order."

"So?"

"The rest of the bookcase. Everything is in order. But these aren't."

She opened the top one. A few of the pages were crumpled as if they'd been hastily shoved back into place.

She frowned, glancing at the window again. If someone had come through that way, they might have knocked the window into the stack of books, scattering them. And then in their haste, they might have returned them improperly.

She nibbled on the corner of her lip in thought and adjusted the brim of her pale hat.

Then she approached the window, took two steps, as if she had just climbed through, and went very still.

Ethan noticed her line of sight. "Oh shit," he said.

Oh shit was right.

A shell casing lay next to the desk, hidden in shadow.

Rachel snapped on a fresh pair of gloves, crouching to get a closer look. Nine millimeter. Recently fired. She straightened, scanning the room.

Dust motes drifted through shafts of sunlight in the stillness. The heavy tang of smoke lingered, acrid and unpleasant.

In the silence, she became aware of a faint grinding sound outside. Machinery. The pumps and generators that kept the oil flowing day and night, an endless rhythm like a heartbeat.

Ethan shifted beside her. "There were no gunshot wounds on the body, right?"

"Right."

"So who fired the shot?"

"Maybe Ms. Beaumont."

"You think our victim shot the killer?"

"I don't know."

Rachel bagged the shell casing, brow furrowed. No sign of blood. No sign of anything else.

So who had left the casing?

Was it completely unrelated?

"What about the cameras?" he said.

"They're off."

"What?"

"No wires. No battery packs. Just for show." She nodded at the ceiling.

He followed her gaze, then blinked in surprise. "Oh. Huh. Shit. Nice call."

She gave him one of her rare smiles, nodding. He was a very cheerful man, and it was a nice improvement to her last partner's glum attitude. Besides, Ethan was nice to look at.

Perhaps it would be alright to keep him around.

Though time would have to tell.

“We should go to the oil fields. They’re only a mile from here.”

“Alright. I’ll drive.”

She shrugged and led the way out of the study, the evidence bag with the small shell casing clutched in one hand.

CHAPTER FIVE

The vast Texas oil fields stretched endlessly into the horizon, broken only by the occasional pumpjack bobbing its head.

Rachel stared at the rust-colored earth, scuffed with boot prints and tire tracks. In the distance, the lights of the ranch flickered against the dusk—an estate carved out of the plains and sustained by the oil that flowed beneath it.

Most of the roughnecks would be hitting the bars about now, washing away the grit and grime of the day. The thought sent a pang of longing through her. It had been a long time since she'd had a drink with friends.

"Ranger Blackwood?" Her partner stood a few paces away, giving her a questioning look. She shook off her reverie and joined him.

Ethan studied the ground, hands in his pockets where he stood by the front door of their vehicle. "No discernible footprints. Tire tracks are a mess. We'll have to get casts, but it looks like multiple vehicles have been out here recently." He glanced at her. "You sure this is where the body was brought in?"

She nodded once.

They'd circled the field three times, each time looking at the fence. A well-maintained fence.

Only three gaps in it that she'd spotted. One obscured by a tangle of shrubs. Another one used by animals to purloin food from the barracks kitchen—on the opposite side of the fields from where the body was found.

And now this spot.

A gap in the fence, parted vaguely, showing a significant amount of foot traffic, suggesting that the workers on the rigs knew about it too.

Cigarette butts scattered across the ground, along with old, discarded beer bottles.

Rachel scanned the area. Her gaze caught on something—a glint of light peeking from beneath a creosote bush. She strode over and crouched down, gingerly brushing away dirt to reveal a silver cigarette lighter.

Ethan came to stand beside her. "Think it's relevant?"

She turned the lighter over in her gloved hands, noting the intricate engraving. "Expensive taste for a roughneck."

"Maybe one of the bosses lost it."

"Maybe." Rachel's gut twisted as she looked over the deserted field.

The towering drill rigs pierced the dusk sky, their mechanical arms swinging methodically amidst the maze of pipelines and storage tanks. Rachel picked her way across the oil-stained gravel, the pungent fumes stinging her eyes.

"The worker found the body near pumpjack fifteen," Morgan said, consulting his tablet. "Just past that separator."

Rachel nodded, picturing the gruesome discovery. She knew these fields—had grown up near their labyrinth of pipe and steel. Now the land held secrets, buried sins.

They slipped through the gap in the fence, preferring not to announce their presence just yet as they approached the pumpjack, its horsehead bobbing steadily against the bruise-colored sky. Rachel noted the lack of caution tape or cops. The crime scene had already been processed, but she needed to see it for herself.

"Hard to believe the perp dragged a body out here unseen," Morgan said, voicing Rachel's thoughts.

She frowned. "An inside job, you think?"

"Maybe. Lot of opportunity in a place like this." His eyes met hers, an unspoken understanding passing between them.

A work boss was standing by the pumpjack, fidgeting with his hardhat. His weathered face creased into a somber expression as they approached. His eyes took them in, and he glanced at the badge flashing on Morgan's belt. The moment he spotted it, he straightened a bit, clearing his throat and rocking back on his heels.

"Morning," Morgan said.

"Feds?" the old head asked.

"Mhmm," Morgan replied, flashing his ever-present smile. Rachel's was a more reserved disposition as she nodded noncommittally in greeting.

"Heard you were comin'. They know you're here at the front office?"

Rachel didn't reply to this. Instead, she said, "You the one who found the body?"

"I was reading sensors," the man replied. He extended a weathered hand stained in grease and ridged in calluses. "John Baker."

"Nice to meet you, John," Rachel said. "Who found the body?"

"My boss. And a rookie. They're still chatting with detectives from PD at the office."

Rachel just nodded. "So you were on the sensors?"

"One of the attendees," he said quickly, as if worried he might somehow be admitting to more responsibility than he was comfortable with. John nodded, his eyes flicking to the pumpjack and a descending drill hole where the body had likely lain. "Never seen anything like it. Christ almighty…" He crossed himself, gaze distant.

Rachel gentled her voice. "We know this is difficult. But can you walk us through how it happened? Any details could help."

John scrubbed a hand over his jaw. "We found her this morning during startup rounds. Saw something on the sensors blocking things." His lips thinned. "No one deserves to go like that."

Rachel pictured it—John's shout of alarm, the shock bleeding to horror. She studied the pumpjack's rhythmic churn, letting John gather himself.

"Notice anything odd the night before?" Morgan asked, quirking an eyebrow.

"Saw nothing. Most were too drunk anyhow."

"How about heard anything?"

"No signs or sounds that night," he said. "But we get all kinds of critters out here. Could've covered up any noises."

Morgan nodded. "Coyotes. We'll check for fur, tracks. Anything else?"

John hesitated. "The night before, we had a pressure drop in sector nine. Sensor blipped but didn't last long." His eyes met Rachel's. "Could've been when she…when it happened."

Rachel committed the sector to memory. "We'll check it out. Thank you, John." She meant it. Witnesses remembered more under kindness than pressure.

John touched the brim of his hardhat. "Ma'am. Anything to catch the bastard who did this."

"Hey, any chance we can see those sensor logs?" Rachel asked. She quirked an eyebrow. "No need to shut things down with a warrant."

He bit his lip and looked about ready to refuse, when Morgan stepped in, smiling amicably. "No worries. We can get a warrant. Could take a couple of days. You don't mind coming in a few evenings, do you? Shouldn't take more than six or seven hours. Maybe ten."

He stared at this, his eyes widening ever so slightly. And with the zeal of someone attempting to get off jury duty, he said, “Er, well… you know. Login is just my name and the word *pass*, lowercase. So… You know. Didn’t hear it from me, though.”

“Sure, sure. Thanks, man.” Morgan clapped him on the shoulder.

John gave another quick nod of his weathered features and then turned away.

Rachel watched him trudge back to the rig, shoulders bowed.

As he left, she pulled out her tablet, entering the info he’d provided.

“We good?”

“I’m in,” she said, scrolling through data logs as they walked. The sector nine sensor had blinked off at 2:47 a.m. two nights prior.

She chewed her lip. It didn’t feel like a coincidence.

Their boots crunched on gravel as they reached the site. An older pumpjack wheezed in the heat, see-sawing methodically amid dry scrub brush. Rachel pictured the killer dumping the body under the relentless mechanical motion. Alone out here, it would have been quick work.

Morgan circled the site, scanning the ground. He shook his head, finding no tracks or signs of disturbance.

Rachel’s gaze snagged on the pumpjack. “Can we stop it for a minute?”

Morgan raised a brow but hit the emergency shutoff. The pump jerked to a halt, the sudden silence ringing.

Rachel approached slowly. The ground beneath was dark and clumpy.

She frowned, glancing back toward the jack they’d come from.

“These two aren’t connected.”

“How’s that?”

“I mean… if this was the first one to trigger the sensors… I was thinking maybe the body was dumped here.” She pointed at the ground. “But ended up there.”

“Yeah. Right?”

“No,” she said. “Look.” She pointed toward a service hatch. “Other side of the rig. The sensors are for separate units. There’s no connection between them.”

“What’s your point?”

She frowned. “If the body was found over there”—she pointed toward the location nearly a hundred yards away and then slowly turned, frowning—“then what the hell triggered the sensors in sector nine?”

“A glitch? Coincidence?”

“You believe in those?”

“Glitches, yeah.”

She shook her head, frowning.

“What are you thinking?”

“I’m thinking maybe we haven’t found everything there is to find in the earth.”

“What?” Morgan blinked at her, his pronounced jawline growing even sharper as he went still. “You mean… like *another* body?”

She shrugged. “Gonna have to shut things down after all… and go digging.”

“Huh. Well, shit.”

CHAPTER SIX

The scorching sun beat down on the barren oil fields, shimmering off the rusty pumpjacks that dotted the landscape. Rachel wiped the sweat off her brow, her boots crunching on the gravel as she walked toward the cluster of officers in the distance.

She tilted the brim of her pale hat back, allowing the breeze to assuage her warm features.

Two bodies lay sprawled on the ground, pale limbs splayed at impossible angles. Blonde hair matted with blood and dirt, tattered sundresses offering no protection from the elements. Bruises already blossoming along their ankles and wrists were visible past the black sludge from the oil.

Rachel swallowed hard, clenching her jaw.

Her hunch had been right.

A body at sensor nine.

Another at sensor twenty-two.

She glanced back toward the oil fields where more police and response vehicles were combing the oil fields. Excavators had been brought up, and cranes were being used to clear paths for the search teams to look for any other hidden corpses.

Three bodies total so far.

Would they find more?

She pulled a pair of gloves from her pocket and crouched beside the nearest victim. Young, maybe early twenties. The calluses on her hands suggested she was no stranger to hard labor.

Rachel traced a finger along the jagged wound slicing across the woman's throat. Deep. Precise. The work of someone highly skilled.

Her stomach churned as she peered at the other body. Nearly identical lacerations. No signs of a struggle. Whoever did this wanted the women immobilized. Vulnerable.

Bile rose in Rachel's throat. She gritted her teeth against the rage simmering inside her.

She stood up slowly, scanning the crime scene with a practiced eye. Somewhere in this sea of chaos lay the clues she needed. The breadcrumb trail to lead her straight to the reaper's door. In the distance, police lights flashed against the azure sky—a chaotic ballet of red and blue.

A figure was approaching them. A middle-aged woman, wearing a scowl as deep as the ridges along her dark brow.

The woman stepped over dusty terrain, frowning at the two of them. When she caught Rachel's eye, she gestured for her to approach.

Rachel picked her way across the rocky terrain, her boots crunching on gravel and sand as she drew near the approaching coroner.

The coroner in question didn't wear a lab coat, didn't look professional. She wore a dusty sweater and sweats.

But Dr. Avery was one of the best in the business, and Rachel had worked with the woman on more than one occasion. The two new bodies lay behind Rachel, discarded like refuse.

"No ID yet," the coroner said as she drew near. "Ran it twice."

Rachel bent down beside the nearest victim. "When can you get them out of here? The manager wants us out of his hair."

"He'll have to wait his turn like everyone else." The coroner sighed, swatting at the flies buzzing around the bodies. "My team is already overwhelmed. It'll be at least twenty-four hours before I can get anyone out here."

Rachel nodded once.

"Anything stand out?" Morgan asked, coming up beside her.

The coroner had come and gone twice already. The first time for a preliminary, the second for pictures. This was her third visit to the corpses, and the thin glaze of sweat across her brow suggested the hike through the sweltering fields was taking its toll.

"Ligature marks suggest he kept them alive for a while," Dr. Avery said. "But the killing blow was quick. Almost merciful."

"Find anything when you ran their faces?" Rachel said.

"Haven't got to that yet," Avery replied, testily.

Rachel noted the coroner's tone but let it slide. The woman was under a lot of pressure. Having worked with Dr. Avery before, she knew the woman was just as overwhelmed and frustrated as the rest of them.

"Let's get their prints and dental records to the lab. See if we can get an ID," Rachel said.

Avery began to reply, but before she could, they were all distracted by shouting.

"One moment, sir!" an officer was saying, standing by a sawhorse a hundred yards ahead. The officer had been stationed to cordon off the scene.

But now, a man was approaching them, shrugging off the officer's hand and striding forward, frowning as if his life depended on it.

And while his life was safe, his livelihood had currently come to a grinding halt.

"Manager?" Morgan guessed under his breath.

Avery just nodded, lips tight.

The manager stormed over, expensive Italian loafers crunching on the gravel. "Do you have any idea how much money you're costing me?" He jabbed a finger at Rachel, then at Morgan, then back at Rachel, as if he were trying to detect *who* exactly he could blame.

The man looked more like a Wall Street broker than a Texas oil field manager with equity in the company. He had sunken features and sun-stained skin, but his thin beard was trimmed in a neat line like a manicured garden outside a dilapidated home.

"Mr. Toney, we're doing everything we can," Rachel said quietly. "But you can't be here right now, sir."

His gaze settled on her now, and his eyes narrowed. Having decided on a target for his ire, he drew in a breath and exclaimed, "I want your badge for this. You're done here!"

Rachel kept her gaze level, refusing to be intimidated. She had faced far greater threats than an irate businessman. "There have been murders on your property. This is now a crime scene, and you will give my team full access until our investigation is complete."

She spoke slowly, firmly, but without attitude. She was simply stating facts, not trying to piss him off or get into a power trip contest.

But he took it the wrong way.

"You can't talk to me like that!" He puffed up, trying to assert his authority, but Rachel didn't flinch. She merely stared at him, as unmoving as a mountain.

"What's your name?" he demanded. "Badge number?"

"Sir," she said quietly, "you're not allowed to be here. You're contaminating my crime scene."

"Like hell I am."

She pointed at his feet, then at the ground behind him. "Size nines," she said simply. "The other tracks were size tens. You've ruined three prints, and the cigarette smoke I can detect on you is going to get on the bodies and show up on her tox screens."

He opened his mouth as if ready to yell some more, but then stiffened as he realized what she was saying.

He frowned deeply.

"What the hell?"

"Yes, sir," she said quietly. "Now please, let us do our jobs."

He sputtered a moment longer, then deflated with a scowl. "You have two days. After that, I'm bringing in my own security team to clear you out." And as quickly as he'd come, he stomped off, leaving Rachel unruffled.

"Nicely handled," Morgan said. A flicker of humor lit his eyes. "I see those stare-downs with charging grizzlies finally paid off."

She glanced at him. "Someone told you about that?"

He smirked. "I wasn't sure it was true until now."

Rachel's lip twitched. "He's less frightening than a hungry bear." Her hands tightened as she gazed at the bodies. "But our killer is another matter. Three victims so far." She glanced at Avery. "Were they all killed at the same time?"

The coroner just shook her head. "Can't give you a definite answer."

"We can't wait twenty-four hours on that," Rachel said.

"I might be able to get someone out here faster," Morgan cut in. "My uncle works for a local hospital."

Rachel blinked. "That's convenient."

He shrugged. "Most of my family is local. Seven brothers. Three sisters." He beamed and winked. "Homeschooled."

She studied him to see if he was joking, but he was just beaming all the more.

She shrugged. "Well, if you can get us someone to take the bodies in, that'd be great. We need to know times of death. And compare them to the heiress."

Morgan nodded, a grim smile touching his mouth. "Well… we can take 'em in, but not process them."

Rachel hesitated, her frown deepening.

"What?"

She glanced off across the desolate terrain. "I… might have an idea," she murmured.

"Yeah?"

"A couple of old friends. Off the rez."

“Don’t know that reservation coroners have jurisdiction here,” said Morgan hesitantly, keeping his voice low and glancing to the cop by the sawhorse.

“Yeah… yeah, we’d have to invite them in special. But they’re good. Really good.”

“I mean… if you think you can sneak them in here, I’m all for it.”

Rachel nodded, giving him a once-over.

“What?” he said.

“Nothing. Just… you’re not a wuss like my last partner.”

“Well… I’ll take that as a compliment. So… who are these coroner friends of yours?”

“Never said they’re coroners.”

“Oh. What are they?”

“Vets.”

“Like as in military vets?”

“No. Veterinarians.”

“Oh.”

Rachel winked at him. “I’ll give ’em a call. Thanks for the backing.”

“I mean… wait. Like puppy and bunny vets? Or like big bear and cool shit vets?”

“I don’t know what that means, Morgan.”

She stepped away, phone rising already. It had been a while since she’d spoken with the Dentons. Close friends of her aunt… She didn’t normally like interacting with people from the rez. Ever since she joined the Rangers, she’d been accused of selling out her own.

But the reason she’d joined was to *help.* How often were Native victims ignored? The crimes against them left unsolved?

She shook her head, summoning a stiff, inner resolve, and placed the call.

CHAPTER SEVEN

Rachel glanced over her shoulder, making sure no one was watching as she carefully lifted the police tape and guided Avon and Magnolia Denton through the fence surrounding the crime scene. The sun was high in the sky, casting a bright glow over the desolate field.

"Thank you for coming on such short notice," Rachel whispered to the couple, both in their fifties and kindly in demeanor. They were local veterinarians who worked for the reservation. Both of them had a clean-cut look about them. And both of them had kind eyes with a distant sort of look, as if they'd seen far too much in the world. The woman, Magnolia, wore a long green dress with a pattern of flowers of many colors. Her hair was long and straight, touching the top of her back. The man wore blue jeans and a short-sleeved plaid button-up shirt. His hair was tied at the back of his head in a ponytail.

"Of course, dear," Magnolia replied. "Whatever you need."

As they approached the two lifeless bodies, the couple exchanged glances, and Rachel could see the concern in their eyes. Despite their primary profession, they were highly educated medical professionals—Dr. Avon Denton held an undergraduate degree in forensic science, while his wife, Dr. Magnolia Denton, specialized in pathology during her veterinary studies.

"Such a tragedy," Avon murmured, kneeling beside the first victim and examining the cuts along the neck.

Ethan Morgan stood off to the side, keeping an eye out in case anyone started questioning the credentials of the two new arrivals. Rachel had instructed him to say they were both CSIs.

Avon's gloved fingers were steady as he gently probed the edges of the lacerations.

"How are things, Rachel?" he said in that familiar, soothing voice of his. A voice developed over nearly three decades working with wounded and injured creatures.

Rachel had often visited the vet clinic during her time on the rez. It had been one of the happy highlights. Many conversations had occurred there—where she'd sat on the hand-carved wooden bench in the lobby, watching passersby bring their distraught creatures through the entrance. She'd felt, in some ways, that those times had been just as healing for her as for the animals.

"Oh, you know," she said conversationally. "Same ol', same ol'."

He glanced up at her. "You givin' me a bullshit answer or an answer answer?" He smiled to show he was kidding.

The familiar phrase evoked a grin of her own. He'd often asked the same question when she'd been younger. An answer answer? Or a bullshit answer?

She said, "Probably a bit of both."

"That's nice," Magnolia said, distractedly.

Rachel could feel Ethan's eyes moving over to them, watching with extreme curiosity. She tried not to look in his direction. It felt vulnerable to reveal these friends of hers, but it was touching that they'd come at a moment's phone call.

"How long's it been since we've seen you?" said Avon. And though his tone was pleasant, there was a note of acerbity in it, like a hint of lemon in a cup of water.

"Oh, huh. Probably three years? Auntie's fiftieth birthday party was the last time, I think."

Magnolia gave Rachel a sympathetic smile. "We'll have to catch up properly soon."

Magnolia knelt by the second body, taking care not to disturb any potential evidence. She looked up at Rachel, concern etched into the lines around her eyes. "How have you been holding up, dear? Did things work out with that Martin fellow? He seemed nice."

Rachel shifted uncomfortably. "Er, no. We broke up not long after that night, actually." She forced a quick nod and offered a tight-lipped smile, deflecting the personal question. "Find anything?"

Magnolia looked down again. She hesitated. "From what I can see," Magnolia began, "the injuries seem consistent with a single-edged blade, likely serrated." She looked up at Rachel. "A lot of knives like that. But these cuts…" She trailed off, shaking her head. Magnolia frowned as she probed the neck wound on one of the victims.

"Something's not right here," Magnolia murmured, sharing a glance with her husband. He looked over, and his brow furrowed.

It was as if the two were communicating telepathically, or perhaps in a language Rachel didn't know.

After the shared glance between the couple, Magnolia continued, "The stab wounds are superficial—they didn't pierce any major arteries or organs."

Avon nodded in agreement. "Neither victim bled out from these injuries. In fact"—he paused as he wiped away some of the dirt around the mouth of one victim, revealing an oily residue—"it appears they were drowned in oil."

He glanced at the large pumpjacks bobbing around them.

"The wounds are superficial?" Rachel asked, perking up.

"Perhaps the killer used the knife as a means to threaten and subdue the victims," Avon speculated, his eyes never leaving the body in front of him.

Rachel considered this possibility, her mind racing with theories. As the Dentons continued their examination, she caught sight of something unusual on the second victim's clothing—a faint dusting of red powder that stood out against the dark stains of oil.

"Did you see this?" Rachel asked, pointing at the red dust. The Dentons looked up from their work and leaned in for a closer inspection.

"Interesting," Magnolia mused. "It looks like mineral deposits, but I can't be sure."

"Could it have come from the surrounding area?" Rachel wondered aloud, scanning the crime scene for any traces of the same red substance.

"No." Avon shook his head. "I've lived here my whole life, and I've never seen anything quite like this. It's definitely not native to the area."

She frowned, took a picture of the red dust, then made a mental note to have forensics sample it.

The Dentons both stood in unison, as if they'd rehearsed the motion. They both dusted their hands off before turning to her.

"Drowned in oil," Avon said simply, shrugging.

"Yeah… thanks," Rachel replied.

"How about you come by for dinner tonight," Magnolia said. "Your aunt will be there!"

"Oh, really?"

"Mhmm. Because I'm going to invite her after we leave here," she said, smiling sweetly with a glimmer of mischief in her eyes.

"Oh. I mean… I wouldn't want to bother you."

"No bother at all."

Rachel didn't like going onto the reservation. The glances she got, the comments she overheard… The sellout. Choosing the white man over her own people. Half-breed. She'd heard it all before.

Now, though, she couldn't refuse. She nodded once, the feather in her hat fluttering. "Alright. Just text me a time."

"Lovely!" said Magnolia. "It's a plan."

Rachel gave a quick nod of gratitude to both of them as she led them away from the crime scene once more, to help usher them out of the oil fields.

She noted the way the two veterinarians held hands as they strolled, both of them occasionally pausing to point out some sight that caught their attention, or a bird flitting on the breeze. They seemed so happy. So unencumbered.

As she watched them, Rachel felt a flicker of… pain? Longing?

She thought of her own parents. And her thoughts darkened, and her usual frown returned, covering her features in an overcast grimace.

She gave a final wave as the Dentons moved off, still holding hands.

"So the wounds weren't the cause of death?" Morgan asked at her side.

"Apparently not," she murmured.

"Well… shit."

"Yeah… But that dust. I want to check it out."

"The dust?"

"Mhmm."

"Right… you used to be a big game hunter for the state, didn't you? Going after predators, right? You seen that dust before?"

She shook her head. "But I have a way of finding it."

She turned and began to move with long strides away from the crime scene.

CHAPTER EIGHT

Rachel's frustration was mounting in the dimly lit precinct interrogation room. She'd been allowed to borrow it from the locals for research purposes, but now, the late-afternoon sun peeking through the single reinforced window above the table almost seemed to be taunting her.

She'd spent over an hour poring over maps and geological surveys of the area, searching for any hint of where the red dust could have originated.

Her eyes were starting to blur, and her head was beginning to ache. She rubbed her temples, pausing to take a deep breath and clear her mind. She couldn't give up now.

Ethan Morgan had dozed off in the chair across from her, his head lolling to the side.

She frowned briefly, staring at the red dust particles in the small plastic baggie sitting on the table next to her.

Her eyes returned to the database open on her computer. Geological samples were compiled on a public works website, and her eyes had glazed over as she kept scrolling through.

The reddish tinge of the dust she'd found on the victim's clothing, accompanied by the faint marks of residual sediment, gave her a unique enough starting point that the venture didn't feel entirely hopeless.

She paused for a moment. She narrowed the soil sample by visual appearance, this time removing any out-of-state results. She had no lab results, so she couldn't narrow by sediment type.

She looked again at the small plastic bag on the desk.

She'd grown up as a hunter.

Had lived in the wilderness, knew this place like the back of her hand.

She opened the soil sample and inhaled the contents.

She ran her fingers over the grains as if she were stroking the fur of some favorite hound.

Soft to the touch. Dry, but not as dry as sunbaked soil. She frowned. Irrigated?

She thought she detected the faint fragrance of petrichor.

She glanced to make sure Morgan wasn't watching, and then dabbed her pinkie against the soil, raising it to her lips. The taste was earthy, slightly bitter, but with a hint of sweetness. No… not sweetness. A soil additive. The sort of additive to help plants grow?

She wiped at her lips and sat back in her chair, her mind racing with possibilities. Irrigation meant agriculture, and the faint fragrance of petrichor hinted at a recent rainstorm.

She pulled up a map of the local farms and began to cross-reference the soil samples with the locations of the farms and recent rainfall.

None.

She sighed, drumming her fingers against the table.

Not rainfall, maybe.

If there was soil fertilizer, and irrigation…

A plant nursery?

She blinked. And then entered the same information, but this time narrowing based on nurseries.

A hit.

She stared, feeling a slow tingle down her spine. She quickly looked up the nursery—Desert Beauty—and found its location near the oil fields where the bodies had been discovered.

She went onto the website and spotted the soil in the potted cactus plants.

She glanced at the packet on the table, then back at the soil. Her eyes widened.

"Shit."

She slammed the laptop lid and surged to her feet.

As she grabbed her jacket and keys, Ethan stirred. "What happened?"

"I think I've found something," she said breathlessly. "You coming?"

He also rose, moving eagerly.

When they reached the car, Rachel rounded on Ethan. "The red dust we found on the bodies? It's used at this nursery called Desert Beauty. It's not too far from here."

"Interesting," Ethan mused. "But why would the killer leave such an obvious clue?"

"Maybe it wasn't intentional," Rachel suggested. "Or maybe they wanted us to find it. Either way, we need to check it out."

He hesitated for a moment before nodding. "Okay, let's do it. But be careful—we don't know what we're walking into."

As they drove to the nursery, Rachel couldn't help but feel grateful for the help she had received from the Dentons. Their expertise had provided valuable insight into the case, and she made a mental note to thank them properly once the investigation was over. The thought of having dinner with them on the reservation gave her no small amount of unease, but she'd cross that bridge when she came to it.

***

The sun dipped lower in the sky, casting an orange glow over the surrounding landscape as Rachel and Ethan stood outside their car, gazing at the small nursery before them. Desert Beauty, a haven for rare cactuses and other exotic plants, was nestled between rocky outcrops and dusty roads on the outskirts of the small town bordering the oil fields. The red dust they had found on the victims, used by the nursery to nurture its unique flora, could be the link they needed.

Rachel scanned the rows of cactuses beyond the fence.

"So… what are we looking for?" Ethan asked, uncertainty flickering across his face.

"Let's start with any employees or customers that might have accessed the location in the last couple of weeks. We need to interview them, dig into their backgrounds, see if anyone stands out."

As they walked toward the entrance, Rachel couldn't help but feel the weight of the investigation bearing down on her shoulders.

"We can't rule out the possibility that this is all just a coincidence, right?" Ethan ventured, his concern creasing his brow.

"I'm aware," she replied, her voice barely more than a whisper.

As they entered the nursery, which was free of customers at the time, Rachel's eyes were immediately drawn to the red dust scattered around the bases of several cactuses, its vibrant hue standing out in stark contrast to the muted colors of the desert. She knelt down, running her fingers through the gritty substance. It had the same scent and texture as the dust from the victim's corpse.

With a nod, Rachel rose to her feet, turning slowly.

And then a voice called out. "You got a lot of nerve coming back here. Hands up, or I'll blow your brains out!"

CHAPTER NINE

Rachel and Ethan slowly raised their hands. Rachel turned warily. A man emerged from behind a cluster of cactuses, a shotgun trained on them. He was tall and wiry, with sun-weathered skin and a wild look in his eyes.

"Who are you?" Rachel asked, trying to keep her voice steady.

"I'm the owner of this here nursery," the man spat. "And you two are trespassing on private property."

"We're with the Texas Rangers," Ethan said, holding up his badge. "We need to ask you a few questions."

The man sneered. "I ain't got nothing to say to no cops." His eyes narrowed, fixating on Rachel. "I seen you here before."

She just watched him. "I've never been here, sir."

"Well… then someone like you fair enough."

She let out a slow breath, lowering her hands.

He kept his gun trained, but didn't react. He looked nervous now, clearly having realized he'd made a mistake, but not wanting to lose face by backing down.

She watched him, a questioning look on her face.

"You thought someone who looked like me had been here before?"

He muttered under his breath. It sounded something like, "Y'all look the same."

Ethan suddenly scowled, his hands lowered now as well. "Lower your weapon," he snapped. "Now!" The ever-present friendliness in Ethan's voice vanished in that moment. She glanced over at him, but he was still glaring at the man with the gun.

Rachel took a step forward, keeping her hands lowered. "We're investigating a murder case, and we have reason to believe that the red dust used in your nursery might be connected."

The man's eyes widened, and he lowered the shotgun slightly. "What are you talking about?"

"Talking about exactly what I said," she replied softly.

She didn't make a big deal about his stereotyping her. She was used to it. The people on the rez saw her as a traitor because she worked with the Rangers. But people outside the res saw her as an outsider.

Not everyone. She'd often found good folk who didn't care a lick. She forced herself to dwell on them rather than men like this.

She wasn't sure she could've stayed sane otherwise.

But it bit. A casual sting that occurred whenever she was confronted by it.

The same sting she received when being excluded by the people she'd grown up with on the rez.

"I ain't heard nothing about no murder," the man said, his sun-bleached features like a wrinkled, worn map. He shrugged. "When was this?"

She didn't reply. Instead, she said, "We need a customer and employee list. Spanning the last two weeks."

He frowned now. "You got a warrant?"

She shook her head. "Do I need one?"

"Yeah. Need a warrant."

"Alright," she said softly. "But I'm going to have to ask you to close down until then."

He stared at her. "What?"

"This might be a crime scene," Ethan cut in, a bit eager again. "Can't have people traipsing over things. Need to shut down for a bit. Shouldn't take long for a warrant. Few days?" he said, glancing at Rachel.

She hid a smirk. "They're pretty busy. Maybe a week? Two?"

"Now wait a minute!" the man with the shotgun exclaimed. "This is my damn livelihood. I can't close down for that long. Are you insane?"

"But we need a warrant," said Rachel, glancing back at him. "Right?"

He paused. Then frowned, suddenly realizing he was being strongarmed. "Ah… shit," he said. "Fine. Wait right here."

He muttered something under his breath as he turned away, and Rachel stiffened at the racial insult.

"Hey!" Ethan snapped after the retreating man, but the fellow with the shotgun pretended he hadn't said anything and continued on his way.

"It's fine," Rachel said, holding Ethan's arm. "Let it go. We're getting what we want."

He looked at her. "You deal with this shit often?"

She nodded. "Mhmm."

He ran a hand through his sandy-brown hair, his eyes flashing above his pronounced cheekbones. Vaguely, an errant thought distracted her. Ethan looked quite… nice… when he was angry.

But she kept the thought to herself as the nursery owner returned, waving a piece of paper like a white flag.

"Here. Customers and employees," he snapped. "Now can you get off my property?"

Rachel took the paper from him, scanning the list quickly. "Thank you," she said, handing it over to Ethan. "We'll be in touch."

The man nodded once, his shotgun still in hand as he watched them leave. Rachel could feel his eyes on her back as they walked away, and she tried to ignore the unease that crept up her spine.

"That was intense," Ethan said once they were back in their car. "You handled it well."

Rachel shrugged, her mind still on the man with the shotgun. "It's part of the job," she said, glancing over at him.

They drove in silence for a few minutes, the tension slowly dissipating. Rachel couldn't help but steal glances at Ethan, taking in the way the sunlight caught on his hair and the rigidity of his athletic frame. She shook her head slightly, trying to clear her mind.

"So, where to next?" Ethan asked, breaking the silence.

Rachel consulted the list of names on her phone. "Gotta narrow the list somehow."

"Could check for priors?"

"Might not be a repeater."

"Could narrow based on age and physical ability. Not easy to lug a body through oil fields."

She nodded and began tapping away at the screen, determined to find *something* to give them a lead.

A monster still lurked in the dark. And they were on his trail.

CHAPTER TEN

The moon hung low in the sky, casting an eerie glow on the deserted street. It was as if nature itself conspired with the darkness within the vehicle.

The truck rumbled to life, drowning out the sound of her whimpers. The victim lay in the back, her once pristine white blouse stained with dirt and sweat, her makeup smeared from her frantic tears. Her chest heaved as she tried to control her breathing, fear clawing at her insides like a feral beast.

He watched her in the rearview mirror, savoring her terror. Studying her fear, the widening of her eyes, the panting breaths.

"Please," she whispered again, her voice barely audible above the growl of the truck's engine. "I have a family."

The man's grip tightened on the steering wheel, his knuckles turning white. He glanced in the rearview mirror again, catching a glimpse of her tearful eyes and trembling form. For a moment, something stirred within him—something alarmingly close to guilt.

"Life," he said quietly, "is a fleeting thing."

As the truck sped into the night, the man felt his pulse race. With each passing mile, the grim reality of her situation would become more apparent, the way it did with *all* of them.

He peered ahead at the dark night roads. He liked to work at night, in the solitude and the quiet.

It was like working in the rain.

The world just seemed… smaller somehow when the streets cleared late at night.

The truck's headlights pierced through the darkness ahead as it sped along the desolate road.

"It won't be long now," he said, hoping to comfort the woman, like a lamb being led to the slaughter.

Suddenly, a flickering red and blue glow appeared in the distance, casting eerie shadows on the surrounding landscape. The driver's heart skipped a beat; a police traffic stop lay directly ahead. Two uniformed officers stood next to their patrol car, scrutinizing one other late-night vehicle before waving it through.

“Damn,” the killer muttered under his breath, his grip tightening on the steering wheel. Sweat beaded on his forehead as he weighed his options. He couldn’t risk turning back now; it would only alarm them. But the thought of being caught with a captive victim in his truck sent chills down his spine.

“Stay quiet,” he hissed at the girl in the back, aware that her pleading eyes were still watching him through the rearview mirror. “Or I swear, you’ll regret it.” He showed her his knife, making sure she had a long look at the rust-stained ridge.

As the truck neared the checkpoint, the man of sorrows’ anxiety reached new heights. Desperation clawed at his insides, threatening to consume him. He wiped his clammy hands on his pants and tried to steady his breathing, reminding himself that he had talked his way out of worse situations before.

He glanced in the back seat, grabbed at the woman’s shirt, and pulled her forward.

She fell into the leg room between the back seat and the front, lodged in the dark, in the shadows.

The seat was now clear.

The car empty.

She let out a faint gasp as she fell, but then went quiet.

For now.

“If I go down,” he whispered, “I’ll cut your throat before they take me.”

She held her breath.

“Evening, Officer,” he said with forced cheerfulness as he rolled down the window. The first officer approached, shining his flashlight into the cab.

“License and registration, please,” the officer commanded, his voice stern and unwavering. The killer fumbled for the documents, careful to keep his trembling hands hidden from view.

“Been drinking tonight?” the second officer asked, leaning in closer to get a better look at the driver. The killer’s heart thumped in his chest, but he managed a convincing smile.

“Water only, I’m afraid. Long drive,” he replied, trying to maintain an air of nonchalance.

“Where you headed?” the first officer inquired, scanning the truck’s interior with suspicion. His eyes moved over the backseat.

But his angle didn’t give him the crucial glance into the leg space between the seats.

"Home. Just finished a delivery," the killer lied, hoping his voice didn't betray his nerves. He had always hated cops.

The officers exchanged glances, their expressions unreadable. For a moment, it seemed as if they might ask to search the truck—an eventuality the killer knew he couldn't afford. His right hand, hidden by his thigh, squeezed tightly around the hilt of his knife. He fought to keep his face neutral, but inside, his thoughts raced with panic and dread.

"Alright, just be careful out there," the first officer finally said, handing back the license and registration. The killer exhaled in relief, nodding his thanks.

As he rolled up the window, he half expected them to change their mind. To try and stop him.

But it didn't happen.

The engine rumbled. The woman whimpered, and then they were moving again. As he drove away, he couldn't help but feel a surge of adrenaline at his narrow escape.

He glanced in the rearview mirror one last time to make sure the police were out of sight before increasing his speed. Fear still coursed through him, compelling him to be extra cautious. He made a conscious effort to obey every traffic rule, taking care not to draw any unnecessary attention to his vehicle.

"Can't afford another close call like that," he muttered to himself as he turned onto a less-traveled road. His thoughts raced with potential escape routes and alibis should the police catch up to him again. He knew he had been playing with fire, and it was only a matter of time before his luck ran out.

As he drove further into the darkness, the quiet was suddenly disrupted by a faint whimpering sound coming from the back of the truck. It was barely audible above the hum of the engine, but the killer's ears attuned to it instantly. The reality of what he had done came crashing down on him as he realized that there was no turning back now.

"Please… let me go," the muffled voice of his captive pleaded softly from the back, her words laced with pain and fear. The killer clenched his jaw tightly at the sound, his guilt intensifying with each passing moment.

"Stay quiet!" he snapped, anger mingling with his remorse. "I'm sorry… I didn't want this," he whispered more to himself than the victim, struggling to reconcile his actions with the person he once considered himself to be. But he was saving them all, wasn't he? It was for everyone.

"Please," he whispered, "I'm sorry."

She let out another sob.

The killer drove on, his mind a whirlwind of emotions as he continued down the desolate road. The night around him seemed darker and more foreboding than ever before, mirroring the turmoil within his soul. With every mile traveled, the weight of his guilt grew heavier, threatening to crush him under its oppressive force. But still, he drove on—deeper into the darkness, with no way to turn back.

The enjoyment he sometimes felt was dwarfed by the shadow of his guilt.

Both emotions warred within him, and he fought to keep himself from changing his mind. From altering the plan.

There was only one path forward. He knew that much.

He nodded, staring ahead toward the glistening metal arms rising and shrugging from desolate fields, streaked by flickers of moonlight.

The earth had to feed.

And he was its provider.

This time, when she whimpered, he didn't feel nearly as bad.

CHAPTER ELEVEN

The fluorescent lights above flickered, casting an eerie glow on the otherwise gloomy precinct break room. Rachel sat hunched over her computer, her fingers flying across the keyboard as she scrolled through the cactus nursery's employee and customer records.

"Come on, come on," she muttered under her breath, her voice barely audible over the hum of the computer fan. "There has to be something here."

Rachel leaned in closer to the screen, meticulously examining each record as if it held the secret to cracking the case wide open. She scribbled down notes, cross-referencing names, dates, and locations of travel records, payment records, credit card records that helped narrow geography.

Ethan sat across from her, frowning at his own computer, his handsome, sharp features illuminated by the glow of the screen in the dingy room.

A bead of sweat trickled down Rachel's temple as she leaned closer to the computer screen. The room seemed to close in around her as she scrolled through the endless rows of names and dates. Her eyes flicked back and forth, reading each line with keen precision.

"Gotcha," she whispered under her breath, excitement coursing through her veins.

"Find something?" Ethan's voice startled her out of her concentration.

Rachel swiveled in her chair to face her partner. "The nursery owner hired a group of day laborers to work there. All of them in the age range we're thinking. Two with criminal records. All with purchases near the crime scenes during our window of opportunity."

"Interesting," Ethan mused, rubbing his chin thoughtfully. She noticed a metal chain around his neck that he sometimes played with. The chain had a crucifix on the end that he kept tucked under his shirt. With his southern drawl, his easy smile, and his apparent religious upbringing, Rachel wondered if the two of them could've been more different from the other.

He'd also mentioned his large family more than once. She'd been an orphan.

It was almost comical they'd been paired together. And yet… she found she liked his company. His eagerness. His direct, unassuming nature. He didn't seem to have a bone to pick with her, and was happy to follow her lead.

"Got names?" he asked.

"I'm running into some hiccups. I think two of them might be brothers. The criminal records are showing up, but under different names. Same socials."

"So they maybe lied about their first names?"

"Yeah."

Ethan leaned back, hands crossed behind his head. "So first we need to find out more about these laborers—where they're coming from, what their backgrounds are, any possible motives."

"Yeah."

"Alright," Ethan agreed, pulling up a chair beside her. "Let's start digging into these guys. We'll cross-reference their information with criminal records and see if anything might be under the aliases they used, too."

"Not this guy," Rachel said suddenly. "Shit. Credit card purchase two hundred miles away the day the first body was found."

"Maybe he gave his card to someone?"

"I doubt he knew we'd look into it if he was as clumsy as all that with his initial spending spree. Near the crime scene."

"Right… so not him. One of the brothers?"

She stared at the screen. Two faces peered back at her. The family resemblance was apparent, but not obvious. The two of them looked like they came from different worlds. One had piercing blue eyes and a chiseled jawline, while the other had dark, brooding features.

Both of them looked world weary and tired.

Mark and Jared Adelman.

She scanned through the names they'd provided to the nursery and then glanced back at their pictures.

"Both involved in an assault five years ago," she said.

"Worth checking out."

She nodded, slowly rising to her feet. It was late now. Very late. Night had fallen, and already she could feel exhaustion weighing heavy on her.

She stifled a yawn even as the thoughts prompted it.

“We got that motel booked?” she asked.

“Don’t you have dinner with your fam?”

Rachel cursed. She’d forgotten all about the invitation. She’d left her phone on silent and quickly raised it. Three missed calls.

“Shit,” she said. “Sorry. I’ll meet back with you here in the morning.”

“No problem!”

She cursed again, pocketing her phone and hurrying out the door, her shoes tapping rhythmically in the empty precinct halls.

CHAPTER TWELVE

Rachel's heart pounded in her chest as she sped down the dusty road. Her worn-in Stetson and durable leather jacket didn't offer the usual sense of protective covering. She felt like a teenager again, rushing home after staying out too late.

The moon was low on the horizon, casting long shadows across the landscape and reminding her that she was running two hours late for dinner with the Dentons and her aunt, Sarah Blackwood. Guilt gnawed at her insides, making her grip the steering wheel tighter.

"Damn it," she muttered under her breath, her deep brown eyes flicking from the winding road ahead to the glowing numbers on her dashboard clock. In the back of her mind, Rachel knew that her tardiness wasn't just about disrespecting her aunt's time; it was another crack in their already tenuous relationship. Her aunt had taught her everything—had been a family to her. For the first decade. Then… things had become strained between them, and always on the same subject.

Rachel's parents. Her aunt's sister had died that night too, but the two of them had never been able to really talk about it without someone's feelings getting hurt.

Rachel still visited. But the visits were quick, and ended in hurt feelings more often than not.

She sighed…

As she turned onto the familiar dirt path leading to her aunt's house—Magnolia had texted that Sarah had offered to host—Rachel felt a knot of anxiety tighten in her stomach. She attempted to take a few calming breaths, but all she could think about was how the evening would unfold. Would Sarah be angry? Disappointed? Or worse, indifferent?

Rachel pulled up to the modest wooden cabin and killed the engine, her heart sinking as she noticed the absence of the Dentons' car. She took a moment to collect herself before grabbing her phone and composing an apology text. Her fingers hesitated over the screen for a split second before sending Magnolia the message: "I'm so sorry I'm late. I'll make it up to you."

Tucking her phone back into her pocket, she sighed and stepped out of the car. The cool evening air brushed against her sun-kissed skin, bringing with it the scents of the surrounding forest and a hint of woodsmoke from the chimney. As she made her way to the front door, Rachel couldn't help but admire the resilience and determination her aunt had shown throughout her life. She lived alone, and yet the place looked as immaculate as ever. The garden pristine.

Despite their somewhat strained relationship, Rachel yearned for a more profound connection with the woman who had raised her—the one who had taught her about survival, self-reliance, and the importance of their shared Native American heritage. But as she rapped on the door, her heart heavy with trepidation and self-recrimination, she couldn't help but wonder if she was feeling up to this meeting.

Rachel's breath came in short puffs as she stood on the porch, her knuckles white from gripping the door frame.

A faint light shone through the window at her side, and above the door was a giant moose head, with antlers stretched like the branches of a tree. A moose, Rachel knew, her aunt had shot personally.

Prompt as ever, and to the point as usual, the moment she knocked, there were two quick steps from inside, approaching the door.

Aunt Sarah opened the door, her hawklike nose and intense disposition more pronounced than ever. She had put on a bit of weight, but had a ruddy, healthy glow to her skin. Her features were plain but watchful, and she had the most beautiful eyes Rachel had ever seen, like deep pools of hazel. Rachel took a deep breath, trying to find the right words, but neither of them spoke for what felt like an eternity.

"Come on in," Sarah finally said, her voice betraying a mixture of resignation and relief. Rachel stepped inside, feeling the weight of their shared history hanging heavily between them.

The cabin's interior was a reflection of Sarah's personality—strong, practical, and deeply rooted in their heritage. A bear rug lay across the wooden floor, while a coyote pelt hung on the wall. Above the door, matching the one on the outside, a second mounted moose head silently observed the sparse yet cozy living space. Rachel's eyes lingered on the turquoise and silver bracelet adorning her aunt's wrist.

"Sorry I'm late," Rachel mumbled, avoiding direct eye contact.

She was a Texas Ranger who'd hunted predators through the most extreme climates, and yet *this* was far more frightening to her than anything.

Her aunt responded with a simple nod, her gaze drifting toward the window that overlooked the vast reservation landscape. The bright moon cast long shadows over the mountains and forests that enveloped their remote corner of Texas.

"Your job keeps you busy, huh?" Sarah asked, her tone neutral but tinged with unspoken disappointment.

"Sometimes too busy," Rachel admitted, her guilt intensifying as she remembered the countless hours spent away from the reservation. Though she had chosen the path of the Rangers, a part of her still yearned for the familiarity and connection she could have found working with the reservation police.

"Tell me about your latest case," Sarah said, changing the subject abruptly.

The two of them stood by the window. Neither of them quite wanting to move, or sit, or do anything, as if frightened any sudden movement might startle the other.

Finally, Sarah blinked first. "Come, sit," she said, matching Rachel's curt manner.

She gestured to the table by the window. Wood-carved—handmade. Sarah had created most of her own furniture.

As Rachel sat, she said, "The Dentons left?"

"Mhmm."

"Shit. Sorry."

"Language."

"Shit—dammit. Wait, no. Sorry."

Rachel bit her lip, feeling like a flustered schoolgirl again in these familiar settings. "I kept the food warm," Sarah said as she placed a steaming plate of frybread, corn soup, and venison stew before her. The scent of the meal filled the air around them, bringing back memories of simpler times.

Rachel shifted uncomfortably at the table, causing the chair legs to move hesitantly across the floor.

Noticing this, Sarah studied her niece. It had been a year since they'd last seen each other? Longer? Rachel couldn't remember anymore.

"Let's eat on the porch," Sarah suggested, her voice gruff yet gentle in its own way. Rachel nodded, gripping her plate tightly as she followed her aunt outside. They sat side by side on weathered wooden chairs, taking in the breathtaking Texas scenery that surrounded them.

"It's beautiful out here," Rachel murmured, trying to break the silence that hung between them. She knew their conversation would likely remain superficial.

"Always has been," Sarah replied, her gaze fixed on the horizon. "But I suppose you don't get to see much of this working for the Rangers."

Rachel's emotions were pained by the seemingly innocuous remark, but she pushed forward, focusing on the weather instead. "The rain's been scarce lately. It's not good for the crops."

"News said there might be a storm coming next week," Sarah said, sipping her broth. "Might help some."

"Maybe." Rachel took a bite of frybread, savoring the familiar taste. They continued to exchange small talk, discussing the latest news and events on the reservation. Each word felt heavy in the air, a reminder that things weren't the same as they used to be. And though Rachel longed for more, she knew better than to push her aunt too far.

"Your job… as a detective," Sarah ventured hesitantly after a while. "How's that going?"

"Busy," Rachel admitted, her thoughts briefly flickering to the lead she'd found on the two brothers who'd worked for the nursery. "There's always something happening."

"Suppose that's true," Sarah said, a hint of pride in her voice. Despite their strained relationship, it was clear she still cared for her niece.

"I'm working on a new case here, bordering the reservation," she said, shifting in her seat to face her aunt.

Sarah raised an eyebrow, clearly intrigued. "Oh? And how's that going?"

"Slowly," Rachel admitted, her gaze falling to the worn planks of the porch. "But it's going."

"Are you still fast?"

"Hmm?"

"Fast," Sarah repeated, scrutinizing her niece. "Like I taught you to be."

Rachel shrugged. "I caught a guy in the woods a few days ago. So yeah. I'm still fast." It sometimes took a moment for Rachel to reacclimate to her aunt's blunt, prying questions. Questions that felt like a planer on wood bark, stripping a tree naked and exposing its vulnerable underbelly.

But they were questions founded in care rather than aggression.

A momentary flicker of pride crossed Sarah's hawklike features, her intense eyes softening ever so slightly. "Glad to know I taught you something worthwhile." She paused, her gaze wandering over the surrounding landscape. "I just wish you'd stayed here, with your people. We could use someone like you."

Rachel felt a twinge of guilt at her aunt's words. "That guy I caught? His victims were Native."

"I see."

"I feel as if I am protecting us."

The older woman didn't respond, her eyes now resting on the distant mountains. Inside the cabin, the pelts that adorned the walls and floor were a testament to Sarah's prowess as a hunter. Her eyes were always searching. The turquoise and silver bracelet glittering on Sarah's wrist had been a gift from her sister—Rachel's mother.

"Sometimes I think about what it would've been like if I had stayed," Rachel confessed, her voice barely more than a whisper. She looked around at the quiet beauty of the reservation and felt a familiar pull in her heart.

Sarah nodded, her expression unreadable.

As they sat there together on the porch, the night sky a vast expanse of darkness speckled with stars, Rachel couldn't shake the feeling that her aunt's approval meant more to her than she'd ever realized. And as the silence stretched between them, filled only by the distant calls of nocturnal creatures, she vowed to do her best not only for herself but also for the people of the reservation—her people.

The wind sighed through the trees, rustling the leaves and carrying with it the scent of pine and sage. Rachel gazed out at the dark landscape and felt a sudden shiver race down her spine, despite the warmth of her leather jacket. She shifted in her seat on the porch, turning to face her aunt, who had fallen silent for a moment.

"Did I ever tell you about the time I saved little Tommy Whitefeather from a mountain lion?" Sarah asked abruptly, her voice roughened by years of harsh living and countless hunting trips. She reached for the rifle leaning against the doorframe, running her fingers lovingly over its worn wooden stock.

"Can't say that you have," Rachel responded, her eyes following the movement of her aunt's hands.

Sarah leaned forward, the lantern above the porch casting shadows across her features as she recounted the tale. "Tommy was only five at the time, playing near the edge of the forest when the cat appeared out of nowhere," she said, her voice tinged with both pride and fear at the memory. "I happened to be nearby, tracking a deer. When I heard his screams, I raced toward him, rifle in hand."

"When was this?"

"A winter ago? Six? I don't know."

"So Tommy is okay?"

"He has a scar to remember the cat by."

"And the cat?"

"He's the carpet in my bedroom."

Rachel hid a smile, shaking her head. Her aunt had always been a force to be reckoned with, and it was in moments like these that she felt the full weight of her legacy.

Sarah pulled a flask from her pocket, unscrewing the cap and taking a swig of whiskey. The amber liquid glowed like captured firelight as she offered it to Rachel, who hesitated for a moment before accepting the drink. The burn of the alcohol seared through her veins, mingling with the lingering chill in her bones.

The two of them sat in silence, watching the distance. It was almost… pleasant.

The unspoken words were painful.

But those that had been shared were comforting in their own fashion.

The cicadas' chorus grew louder as the night settled in, their rhythmic hum punctuating the heavy silence that had fallen between Rachel and her aunt. Sarah's head lolled forward, her breathing slow and steady as she succumbed to the gentle rocking of the chair and the whiskey's warm embrace.

Rachel rose quietly, retrieving a wool blanket from inside the cabin. She draped it over her aunt, tucking it carefully around her shoulders. The scent of cedar and earth clung to the fibers, mingling with the faint aroma of sage that still lingered on her aunt's skin.

Sarah stirred, her lips moving to form words. "You should've long since solved your parents' murder," she mumbled, her voice slurred and thick with sleep.

The words hung in the air like smoke, choking Rachel with a familiar cloud of guilt and frustration. She swallowed hard, her throat tight as she turned away, the floorboards creaking softly behind her.

She wasn't sure if her aunt was even conscious of what she'd said.

But the accusation was one that had been levied in the past.

She just glanced at her aunt, sighed, nodded, then began to move down the steps toward her waiting car. The gravel crunched beneath Rachel's boots as she made her way down the dirt road, her gaze drawn to the silhouette of her car.

She slipped into the vehicle.

"Damn it," she muttered under her breath, her knuckles white as she gripped the steering wheel, her heart pounding in time with the thrumming engine as it rattled to life.

The drive to the motel was a blur, the landscape slipping by like shadows in the moonlight. As the miles passed, memories of her parents floated to the surface, their laughter and warmth filling the hollow spaces within her. She thought of her mother's gentle touch, her father's strong arms wrapped around her as they danced together in the kitchen.

She scowled. She had to find out what had happened to those women.

Tomorrow morning would provide the light. She would just have to follow the trail.

CHAPTER THIRTEEN

The nightmare of her parents' disappearance came quickly, as soon as her head had hit the pillow. Rachel jolted awake, her body drenched in sweat. She could feel her heart pounding against her ribcage as if it were trying to escape. Grasping for air, she tried to steady her breathing, but the nightmare still clung to her like a second skin.

"Damn it," she muttered, wiping beads of perspiration from her forehead. The thin motel sheets were tangled around her legs, and she kicked them off with an irritated groan. Her trembling hands betrayed her attempt at steadying herself.

She squeezed her eyes shut, willing the images from her dream to fade away. Instead, they sharpened, transporting her back to that fateful night when everything changed.

The shattered windowpane was the first thing she noticed. Large shards of glass littered the hardwood floor, their jagged edges glinting menacingly in the moonlight. It was a big window, perhaps four feet wide and six feet tall—large enough for someone to crawl through without much effort.

"Mom? Dad?" Ten-year-old Rachel's voice was barely a whisper, fear constricting her throat. Her small hands trembled as she reached out to touch the broken window, pausing when she saw the blood smeared across the few remaining glass panes. It looked thick and dark, almost black in the dim light. There wasn't a lot of blood, just enough to indicate that whoever broke in had likely cut themselves on the sharp glass.

"Please… please be okay." The plea escaped her lips before she even realized she'd spoken aloud. She blindly felt for the wall, using it to guide her down the hallway toward her parents' bedroom.

"Mom, Dad, are you—" The words caught in her throat as she pushed open the door, only to find the room empty. The bedsheets were thrown back in haste, as if her parents had been ripped from their sleep. But there was no sign of them, no indication of where they could be.

"Where are you?" she whispered, her voice shaking as much as her body.

Back then, she had been wide-eyed and curious, her spirit unbroken by the tragedy that would later define her. She remembered how she'd cling to her Aunt Sarah, the only family she had left after that fateful night, finding comfort in her presence.

Over the years, she developed a thick skin, channeling her emotions into her work and adopting an analytical approach to problem-solving. Her mind became a fortress, guarding her against the shadows of her past.

The motel room was bathed in the pale glow of moonlight, casting eerie shadows on the walls. Rachel lay in bed, her body tense as she fought to silence the fear that gnawed at her insides. She squeezed her eyes shut, trying to banish the images that haunted her, but they refused to be silenced.

"Please… not again," she whispered, her voice trembling. As if in response, the nightmare began anew, clawing its way through her consciousness and dragging her into its inescapable clutches.

Her parents' faces flickered before her, their eyes filled with terror and pain. The sound of shattering glass pierced the air, followed by the sickening splatter of blood. Rachel felt her stomach churn, bile rising in her throat as the horrifying scene unfolded once more. Desperation gripped her, tightening around her throat until every breath was a struggle.

"Stop it!" she cried out, her voice ragged and raw from the effort of holding back her tears. "Please, just stop!"

But the nightmare only intensified, the broken window looming larger than life in her mind's eye. Crimson blood stained the jagged shards of glass, the gruesome remnants of her parents' last moments. Fear, sadness, and frustration roiled within her, a tidal wave threatening to sweep her away.

She buried her head in her pillows, closing her eyes.

She'd been tempted in moments like these.

To drink.

To numb.

But she'd seen what that could do to people.

Had seen what it had done to her aunt.

No…

No, she wouldn't let the waves of emotion toss her about.

And so she suffered.

Lying in bed, motionless, staring at the ceiling.

How often had she tried to solve her parents' case? Suspects had been those opposed to interracial marriages between Native Americans and whites. They had run through the suspects rather quickly.

A cold case.

Nearly twenty years had passed since then.

Rachel had grown up as an orphan. She lay there, breathing heavily, thinking about Ethan.

A man who couldn't have been more different than her. He'd grown up in a large family, with small-town, religious roots.

He'd known what it was to have community. He'd been raised by his parents.

She shivered, trying not to feel the rising sense of envy that thoughts like this often brought forth.

She lay sweating on her sheets like a cornered animal—it was always worse at night, when the dark things came out to play.

Rachel sat up, running her hand through her hair. She knew she wouldn't be able to sleep for an hour, maybe more, not with the nightmare still clinging to her like a bad smell. She needed to do something, anything, to get her mind off the past.

With a sigh, she reached for her laptop, flipping it open. She scrolled through her emails, ignoring the stack of unread messages from her boss.

The case was still tugging at her thoughts.

It was all so much to handle.

She closed her eyes, releasing a pent-up sigh, leaving the lid of her laptop open, allowing the glow from the screen to serve as a nightlight.

A full-grown woman. A hunter, a tracker. A killer.

And yet she needed a damn nightlight to dose off.

But she wouldn't drink.

She wouldn't fall into the trap.

No… no, she'd take the light for now.

She closed her eyes again, flopping back against the bed in some small defeat.

A killer was still out there.

Lurking.

More than one.

Predators came in all shapes and sizes. But she was determined to find this sicko. This man who was dumping women in the oil fields.

Her eyes narrowed, and she leaned back, loosing a pent-up sigh at the ceiling.

Where was the killer now?

Her mind wandered… she wondered what he was up to… Was he worried about her? Could he feel the cops coming closer?

Or were they so far away that their presence didn't even register?

CHAPTER FOURTEEN

The night was alive with the ominous hum of insects as the man perched on the roof of his RV, his legs crossed beneath him. He wore nothing—naked and alone at night, perched on the cold metal.

It was nearly two in the morning, but sleep eluded him, chased away by a gnawing sense of urgency. He couldn't shake the feeling that the end was near, and it was up to him to appease the wrathful earth.

Two half-empty bottles of car oil sat beside him like silent sentinels, their dark contents eerily glistening in the moonlight. The cool breeze carried the scent of oil and cactus to his nostrils, a strange and heady reminder of his twisted mission.

"Must… cleanse myself," he whispered into the night, his words carried away by the wind like some ancient incantation. His hands trembled as he reached for the first bottle, unscrewing the cap with slow, deliberate movements.

"Must… please the earth," he continued, his voice barely audible above the rustle of nearby shrubs. An almost reverent expression settled on his features as he raised the bottle toward the sky, a silent offering to the forces he believed were guiding his actions.

With a sudden, swift motion, he upended the bottle over his head, letting the viscous oil cascade down his face and body. Shivers wracked his frame, not just from the chill of the liquid but from something deeper within him—an ecstatic thrill at the thought of purifying himself for what was to come.

The oil dripped from his chin as the killer's gaze remained fixed on the vast expanse of the night sky above him. He muttered to himself in a hushed tone, each word charged with the weight of his conviction.

"Whispers… whispers from the clouds," he stammered, eyes darting between the stars as if searching for a hidden message. "Tell me how to save us."

A gust of wind rustled the saguaro cacti that surrounded his RV, their spiny arms reaching toward the heavens like twisted worshippers in the moonlit glow. The dark outlines of the oil fields lay beyond, a testament to mankind's never-ending thirst for resources. To the killer, this desolate landscape was both a sanctuary and an omen, a stark reminder of the earth's fragility and the destruction wrought by human hands.

"Must… listen," he urged himself, straining to hear the whispers he believed were carried on the wind. "Must… understand."

He clambered to his feet, swaying slightly as he attempted to find his balance atop the RV. A sense of urgency pulsed through him, driving him to desperation in his search for answers.

"Speak to me!" he cried out into the darkness, hands raised in supplication. "I am your servant! Guide me!"

Silence greeted his plea, and for a moment, doubt flickered across his face.

"Show me the path…" he whispered, his body trembling with anticipation.

In that instant, it all became clear: the sacrifices he must make, the pain he must inflict, the lives he must take to restore balance. His heart raced as the realization took hold, adrenaline surging through his veins like a tidal wave.

"Thank you," he breathed, voice almost lost in the wind. "I will not fail you."

As the final words left his lips, the killer clenched his fists, steeling himself for the bloodshed to come. He glanced once more at the saguaro cacti and oil fields that stretched out before him—this desolate landscape that bore witness to his twisted calling—and knew that one day soon, they too would be cleansed by the righteous fury of the earth.

The stars above seemed to mock him, their cold indifference piercing through the veil of night. He had always been afraid of nature and the sky, but he could not escape them. They were omnipresent, looming over him like a dark specter from his past.

"Is this what you want?" he muttered, his voice a barely audible whisper as it was carried away by the wind.

A sudden rustling sound caught his attention, and he turned his gaze toward its origin. A small squirrel had appeared on the roof, its eyes gleaming with curiosity. Despite the gnawing fear in his gut, the killer couldn't help but feel a pang of empathy for the tiny creature.

"Ah, you must be hungry," he said softly, reaching into his pocket and pulling out a small wrapper with the remnants of a protein bar. It smelled vaguely of peanut butter, and he tore off a stale piece.

He extended his hand, palm up, offering the food to the squirrel. With tentative steps, the squirrel approached, sniffing the nut-scented bar before taking one corner gingerly in its mouth. The killer couldn't help but smile at the sight; even in a world shrouded in darkness, there was still a glimmer of innocence to be found.

"Enjoy your meal, little one," he murmured, watching as the squirrel scampered back down the RV to snack on its prize.

As the squirrel disappeared into the shadows, the killer's thoughts returned to his own twisted path, his heartbeat quickening with anticipation. He knew what he had to do—the time had come to face his fears and carry out his plan.

"Forgive me," he whispered, his words swallowed by the wind as it swept across the desolate landscape. "I know not what I do."

CHAPTER FIFTEEN

The following morning, Rachel and Ethan found themselves driving through the outskirts of town, their unmarked police car blending seamlessly with the traffic. The sun had barely risen, casting long shadows over the desolate streets as the first hints of daylight filtered through the clouds.

"So his brother's really in prison?"

"Mhmm."

"So it can't be him."

"No. But Mark is out."

"Gotcha," Ethan said. "So this Mark guy had means, opportunity, motive, and a record?"

"Looks like."

"Shit, alright then."

"According to his file, this guy's been living at the Desert Palm Motel for the past month," Rachel said, squinting at the GPS on her phone. "Looks like we're getting close."

A shabby, run-down motel soon came into view, its neon sign flickering weakly in the faint light. As they pulled into the nearly empty parking lot, Rachel couldn't help but feel a sense of foreboding. The place radiated despair, its dark windows staring back at her like soulless eyes.

"Room 107 should be just around the corner," Ethan murmured, scanning the row of doors as they stepped out of the car.

"Stay sharp," Rachel warned, her hand instinctively resting on her holstered weapon. She felt the weight of it against her hip, a reminder of the danger that could lurk behind any door.

"Always am," Ethan replied with a reassuring smile, his own hand hovering near his gun.

As they approached Room 107, the air seemed to grow colder, the silence more oppressive. Rachel's thoughts drifted to her aunt, and the uncomfortable interaction the previous night.

The accusation about her parents' unsolved murders still hung heavy.

But instead of allowing her mind to linger on such things, she steeled herself and focused on the task at hand.

"Ready?" Ethan asked, his hand poised to knock on the door.

"Let's go," Rachel whispered, her eyes fixed on the peeling paint of the motel room door.

Ethan's knuckles rapped against the door with a sense of urgency, the sound echoing in the dimly lit motel hallway. Rachel's heart pounded in her chest, each beat reminding her of the importance of this moment.

"Rangers," she called out firmly, hoping that the announcement would prompt some sort of response.

But there was only silence.

"Give it another second," Rachel whispered, her ears straining for any sign of movement behind the door.

And then, almost imperceptibly, they heard it: the faint sound of shuffling, followed by the creak of floorboards under shifting weight.

"Someone's in there," Ethan murmured, his eyes meeting Rachel's.

She nodded, her mind working quickly as she considered their options. A thousand questions swirled in her head, but one thing was for certain—they couldn't let this opportunity slip away.

"Let's give it one more shot," she decided, raising her hand to knock again. "If they don't answer, we'll have to think of another way in."

Ethan nodded, his expression serious and resolute.

"Rangers! Police!" Rachel shouted louder this time, pounding her fist on the door. "Open up! We need to talk!"

Again, the response was nothing more than quiet, muffled movement. Whoever was inside clearly had no intention of willingly answering the door. Rachel's thoughts raced as she considered their next move, her instincts and training guiding her through the possibilities.

"Alright," she said, turning to Ethan with a determined look. "We're going to have to find another way in. Let's circle around and see if there's a window or something."

"Right behind you," Ethan agreed.

They moved along the side of the unit and approached a window about eight feet off the ground.

Unable to contain her growing impatience, Rachel reached into her jacket pocket and pulled out a small leather case containing a ratchet and pick. The worn case was a testament to the countless times she had relied on these slim metal instruments in her line of work. With a nod from Ethan, she began to work on the lock, her fingers expertly maneuvering the picks as if they were extensions of her hands.

"Cover me," she whispered, her focus entirely on the task at hand.

"Got it," Ethan replied softly, positioning himself beside her and blocking her from the view of the sparse parking lot.

Rachel's pulse raced as she felt the first tumbler click into place, followed by another and then another.

"Almost… got it," she muttered, feeling the final tumbler give way. With a quiet click, the lock disengaged, and the open window beckoned them forward into the unknown.

They slipped into a small bathroom, one at a time. Rachel first, dropping onto the cold, wet tile floors. Ethan came a second later.

Both on the alert, they approached the door to the bathroom, ears attentive, hands on their weapons.

They shared a look. "Ready?" she mouthed.

He nodded once.

They burst into the room, guns drawn and senses on high alert. Every fiber of their being was tuned in to the environment around them, searching for the slightest hint of danger or deception.

"Rangers! Don't move!" Rachel barked, scanning the dimly lit space for any sign of the elusive worker.

"Hands where we can see them!" Ethan added, his weapon trained on the shadows that danced across the walls.

As their eyes adjusted to the darkness, they took in the sparse, dingy room. It reeked of desperation and despair.

"Over there!" Ethan suddenly called out, pointing toward a corner where the shadows seemed to shift ever so slightly.

"Show yourself! Now!" Rachel demanded, her voice firm and commanding.

Silence filled the air, heavy with tension and fear. And then, as if sensing the futility of further concealment, the hidden figure emerged slowly from the darkness—hands raised in surrender, but eyes filled with defiance.

The room was suffocating; the dim light cast by the flickering bulb seemed to gather in the corners, all but swallowed by the shadows. Rachel's fingers twitched at her side as her eyes swept over the sparse furnishings. A single bed, rumpled and worn, sat against the far wall, its sheets stained with the weight of countless forgotten stories. Beside it, a small table listed precariously, one leg shorter than the others. The few personal belongings scattered about only served to amplify the emptiness of the space.

The denizen of the gloomy establishment emerged cautiously from behind the curtain where he'd been hiding.

He was wearing a white T-shirt and boxers. His shirt was stained, his face unkempt. His appearance was that of a man who had given up on himself and the world around him. He stood there, hands still raised, eyes locked on the Rangers with defiance.

"Mark Adelman?" she demanded.

His dark features flickered, and his scowl deepened. "Don't move," she cautioned.

He didn't, still glaring at them. He still hadn't said a word.

"Rachel, look at this," Ethan called out, holding up a crumpled piece of paper he'd snatched from the end table. "A receipt from the nursery—dated just days before the first killing."

"Good find." Her eyes never left Mark.

His stayed on her as well.

Finally, Mark spoke. "What's this about?"

His was a high-pitched, nasally voice. It had an unctuous note in it, and he shifted foot to foot, watching them intently.

"You know," Ethan said scornfully.

Mark looked at them, then flashed a nervous smile. "The murders?"

Ethan went still. Rachel stared.

CHAPTER SIXTEEN

Mark nodded, his head bobbing up and down. "It is about those, isn't it? The murders, I mean."

"What do you know about the murders?" Rachel said cautiously. Normally, suspects didn't just come out and admit their role in a crime.

But there was a first time for everything.

"Not—not much. Heard about 'em on the news."

"Looks like you're packing your bag," Rachel said, nodding across the room. "You going somewhere?"

"Uh, yeah," he stammered, attempting to flash a crooked smile. "Just taking a little trip, you know?"

Rachel ignored his attempt at small talk.

"You worked at a cactus nursery at one point, didn't you? Know the place?"

She didn't use the name, hoping to trap him into volunteering the information. So in any future debriefs he couldn't deny knowledge of their lead.

But Adelman looked at them hesitantly, wrinkling his nose.

"Look, I don't know anything about that," he insisted, his voice cracking ever so slightly. "I was just minding my own business when—"

"Save it," Ethan interrupted, his eyes narrowing with suspicion as he took a step forward. "We know you're involved. Just tell us what we need to know, and maybe we can help you."

For a moment, the room was filled with tense silence.

Rachel eyed Mark warily as he attempted to regain his composure. He flashed her and Ethan a crooked smile, trying to exude an air of nonchalance that was at odds with the beads of sweat dotting his brow.

"Quite the heat wave we're having, huh?" he said, attempting to divert the conversation toward small talk. "I heard it's supposed to be a record-breaker."

Rachel's mouth tightened into a thin line, unimpressed. Those nervous ticks and forced smiles were as transparent as water.

Mark licked his lips nervously, his eyes darting between Rachel and Ethan as if searching for a way out. The anticipation in the room grew thicker, suffocating, like the humid air outside. But beneath Rachel's calm exterior, her mind raced with possibilities.

He was acting guilty. But guilty of what?

That was the question.

His shoulders slumped. And for a brief minute, it almost looked as if he were going to crumple in on himself.

Rachel watched him closely.

"Alright, alright," he conceded, his voice faltering. That's when his hand slipped down to his waistband, fingers trembling as they wrapped around something hidden from view.

"Don't do it!" Rachel said sharply. Her own weapon raised.

But he ignored her. In one swift movement, he produced a rusty revolver, the metal glinting menacingly under the flickering fluorescent light.

He hadn't hit the safety, though. She could see it from here.

So as he raised the gun, she held her fire, hoping Ethan saw it too.

"Stay back!" Mark warned, his eyes wild with fear or perhaps desperation. "I won't hesitate to use this thing!"

Rachel's heart hammered in her chest, her instincts screaming at her to react. But she knew better than to let her emotions take over; the safety was on. His hand was shaking.

"Put it down," she ordered, her voice steady despite the adrenaline coursing through her veins. "You don't want to make things worse for yourself."

From the corner of her eye, she saw Ethan tense, ready to spring into action if necessary. But Rachel hoped it wouldn't come to that.

"Please," she added, softer now but no less determined. "We can still work this out peacefully. I know people like you. One thing leads to another. It all just gets away from you, doesn't it? You didn't mean to hurt anyone. I know that."

Mark's grip on the revolver wavered, his entire body trembling like a leaf caught in a storm. The seconds ticked by agonizingly slow as they awaited his decision, the air in the room heavy with anticipation.

The stale air in the motel room grew even heavier as Mark's shaking hand tightened around the rusty revolver. Rachel watched him carefully, her heart pounding in her ears but her expression calm and steady. She knew that a single wrong move could spell disaster for both her and Ethan. Especially if their suspect noticed the safety was still on.

Fortunately, Ethan seemed to notice the same thing. She spotted, out of the corner of her eye, as he tensed, staring. He inhaled shakily.

He muttered, “Safety,” under his breath.

She nodded a single time, trying not to draw attention to herself.

In a heartbeat, Ethan sprang into action, his athletic body moving with precision and speed. He closed the distance between himself and Mark Adelman in an instant, his hand shooting out to grip Mark’s wrist tightly. With a swift twist, he forced Mark’s arm to bend at an unnatural angle, causing the man to yelp in pain and drop the weapon. The gun clattered to the floor, its hollow sound echoing throughout the room.

“Damn it!” Mark cursed under his breath as he stepped back from Ethan, clutching his injured wrist. His eyes darted around the room like those of a cornered animal, searching for a way out of the situation he’d just made worse for himself.

“Should’ve listened when I told you to put it down,” Rachel said coolly, keeping her gaze locked on the now disarmed man.

“Easy for you to say,” Mark spat, his voice tinged with bitterness and desperation. “You don’t know what I’ve been through, what they’ll do to me if I talk!”

Ethan straightened up, keeping a watchful eye on Mark, while subtly positioning himself between the man and the door. “What *who* will do to you?”

“I—” Mark hesitated, his face a mixture of fear and indecision. As he glanced back and forth between Rachel and Ethan, his resolve seemed to waver.

Rachel took a slow and measured breath. She knew that they were on the precipice of something crucial, and it was up to her and Ethan to ensure that they didn’t slip up. With a quiet determination, she said, “We need you to be honest with us, sir.”

In a split second, Mark’s eyes locked onto the window behind him. The pane was damaged, its jagged edges betraying the motel’s age and neglect. Without another word, he lunged for it, desperation fueling his every move.

“Stop!” Rachel shouted, her pulse quickening as she reached for him. But it was too late. Adelman crashed through the fragile glass, the sound of shattering echoing throughout the room. Shards of glass cascaded to the pavement below like a deadly rain.

Ethan and Rachel exchanged a quick glance, their expressions a mixture of shock and determination. They rushed to the window, hearts pounding in their chests. Rachel peered out the window. Mark was rolling to his feet, sending a shower of glass falling around him.

"Damn it!" Ethan muttered under his breath, frustration clouding his voice. He gripped the windowsill tightly, knuckles turning white.

He flung himself after their suspect, vaulting the windowsill.

Rachel clambered through a second later.

They broke into a sprint, racing down the concrete sidewalk outside the motel.

"I didn't do anything!" Mark was squawking. "Help! Abuse! Police abuse! HELP!"

He ran fast, arms pumping, but he was lagging as he ran. His round belly and unkempt frame didn't aid him in his effort to sprint away.

His eyes glanced frantically around, and he spotted the swimming pool attached to the motel, behind a black gate.

Closed for the morning.

But he ignored the sign, vaulting the fence.

Rachel and Ethan chased after him at a breakneck sprint.

As they got closer to the pool, Ethan paused. A long hose trailed from one side of the pool toward them, the end just outside the fence. He snatched the hose and pulled it taut. It leapt up, and Mark nearly tripped. He yelped and stumbled forward, but his footing became unsure. His shoes skidded on the wet concrete surrounding the pool, and he lost his balance. He fell hard into the pool with a loud *splash!*

Rachel and Ethan both vaulted the fence and skidded to a stop at the edge of the pool, their guns trained on the gasping man as he thrashed around in the water.

"Don't move," Rachel said simply. "Hands where we can see them."

He gasped a couple more times, fear in his eyes, but then he let out a desperate exhalation. And, limping over to the side of the pool, he rested his elbows on the ledge, hands in the air in a posture of defeat.

But there was something in those eyes that Rachel didn't like. And the question still hung heavy… had he killed the women? Was this their man?

She met those eyes and felt a tremor down her spine.

CHAPTER SEVENTEEN

Rachel's boots echoed down the hallway as she led Mark into the interrogation room back at the precinct. The dim overhead lights cast a cold, sterile glow across the cramped space. Mark's wet clothes squelched with every step, a reminder of his recent misadventure in the pool. He had a sullen expression on his face—a far cry from the defiance he'd exhibited back in the motel room.

"Take a seat," Rachel ordered, her tone sharp and authoritative. She didn't have time for pleasantries; there was a murderer on the loose.

Mark slumped into the hard metal chair, his greasy T-shirt clinging to his out-of-shape body. A faint odor of sweat and stale beer wafted through the air, and Rachel fought the urge to wrinkle her nose.

The interrogation room was small, barely enough space for the table that separated her from Mark. A single window punctured one wall, but the blinds were drawn, cutting off any connection to the outside world. On the other side of the table, a large mirror reflected their images back at them—a silent witness to what was about to transpire. Ethan was on the other side, and he'd be making notes of everything, unseen behind the glass. They'd decided to have Rachel approach this on her own to start.

"Let's get started," Rachel said, her deep brown eyes locked onto Mark's unshaven face.

"Tell me about the night of the murders," Rachel said. "Where were you?"

Mark shifted in his seat, avoiding her gaze. "What murders?"

"You'll have to try to be more convincing than that. Where were you two nights ago?"

"I was at home, watching TV," he muttered, picking at a loose thread on his damp T-shirt.

"Can anyone vouch for that?"

"No," he admitted with a sigh. "I live alone."

"Then you can understand why I'm here, asking you these questions. Do you often work for the cactus nursery?"

"What?"

"Just answer the question."

"Look, I didn't kill anyone," Mark blurted out, desperation seeping into his voice.

"You pulled a gun on two Rangers," she said. "And then ran."

He muttered something under his breath.

"What was that?"

"I didn't work for the nursery."

"Liar. We found red dust on one victim that matched the soil samples from the cactuses. And your name is on the employee list."

He stared at her. Opened his mouth, closed it again.

"I didn't end up working there," he said simply.

"I don't believe you."

"I mean, fine… I worked a *bit.* But that was it."

Her voice hardened. "You seem to keep changing your story."

"I worked for a few days, but got canned, alright?"

"Why?"

"I… just… you know, *did.*"

"Without cause?"

He shifted uncomfortably, his sweaty shirt bunching up under rolls of fat. He picked at the shirt with trembling fingers, and then shrugged and mumbled something.

"Louder, please."

"I was skimming money from my boss," Mark confessed, his face flushing. "Just a little bit here and there. I never thought it would amount to much."

"Only one person fits our profile who worked at that nursery. I know about your criminal record," Rachel observed, her tone cool and detached.

Rachel studied Mark's face for a moment. He didn't reply, staring at his fingers.

"Mark, I'm going to show you some pictures now," she said, her voice steady. "I need you to look at them and tell me if you recognize the woman in them."

She reached for the folder and opened it, revealing a series of photographs of the third dead woman they'd found, her body covered in oil. As she spread them out in front of Mark, Rachel watched his face closely, searching for any sign of recognition or guilt.

Mark stared at the images, his eyes widening in horror. "That… that's awful," he muttered.

She studied him. The first victim they'd found had been a billionaire heiress. The next two victims hadn't yet been identified, but the going theory was that someone was targeting the elite.

"I need you to tell me who she was," Rachel said, still watching their suspect's expression.

He was scratching with a dirty finger at his stubble, frowning down at the pictures. His initial repulsion was replaced by a grim sort of satisfaction.

He seemed mesmerized by the sight of it. Rachel said, "Four years ago, you beat a woman with a tire iron, didn't you?"

He blinked, looking up.

"What was her name again?"

He just shrugged, shaking his head. "I didn't do this," he said, pushing the pictures back toward her.

"But you know who she is?"

"No."

"So how come she was at the nursery then? Who else would've attacked her?"

"Might've been a customer. Doesn't mean I killed her."

"No. No, it doesn't, you're right." Rachel paused, and she felt like a lioness with the scent of prey. She could detect some scent on the breeze. A big heap of bullshit.

"You did know her," she tried. And then she lied. "We have security footage of you two together in the parking lot."

He looked at her. "Not possible," he retorted. "Those cameras are for show."

She pointed at him. "Interesting. Someone who hadn't been with the woman might've said it wasn't possible *because it didn't happen.*" She allowed iron to creep into her words again.

He stared at her, mouth agape. "I… just…" He stammered a bit more.

Then he hung his head. "Fine. Fine!"

She felt her pulse quicken.

He raised his head under the lights above. "Yeah. Okay. Fine. I admit it. I met her a couple times. But it was all consensual."

"You slept with her?"

"That's what you do with hookers, isn't it?"

"Hang on, what?"

He blinked. "You don't know? Really. She's a whore. A prostitute. Look." He reached for his phone, which was on the table between them, and hastily unlocked the device and maneuvered to a website. "Low-End Escorts," he said simply. "See?"

He turned the screen toward her. A photo of a figure in black lingerie, smiling at the camera with a too-white, photo-edited smile.

It was hard to tell at first. But the beauty mark on the cheek matched. The facial symmetry matched. It was the same woman.

Rachel stared at the name. *Candy.*

She leaned back frowning, crossing her arms. "So you hired a rent girl and she showed up at the nursery where you were working?"

"I wasn't the only one who had fun with her!" he retorted. "We all chipped in."

"The boss too?"

"Yeah. Was his idea!"

Rachel sighed. "You seemed to find that website really quick."

He mumbled something and shrugged.

Now her mind was racing. He'd connected himself with the victim. But the woman didn't match the initial assumption. A prostitute? Certainly not another heiress…

So who was the killer targeting?

And was Mark Adelman telling the truth?

She looked at him.

He could detect the suspicion in her gaze judging by his next comment. "I can show you! I wasn't the one who drove off with her!"

"How's that?"

"Her pimp picked her up. After. She services oil workers. Lotta interest with itinerants too."

"You can prove it how?" she said waspishly.

He turned his phone to her again, showing her a video. It was a cringe-inducing home movie. Inappropriate for the first few minutes, and Rachel tried to only watch the faces involved.

But then the sexual escapades were interrupted by a loud, barking voice.

The camera panned, turning to spot a large, muscled man with multiple tattoos striding toward them.

"Time's up!" the man was saying. "You only paid for the hour."

There was some grumbling from the camera's speakers, but then reluctant motions.

The woman hastily got dressed, grabbed a small purse, took a couple of bills from the men in question, and, adjusting her miniskirt, hastened toward the large, musclebound goon.

Rachel leaned in, studying the image. The footage was grainy as the two figures moved off in the direction of a waiting car.

She couldn't make out the license plate, but the make and model were clear enough. Rachel jotted down the details in her notebook, then turned back to Mark.

"You're telling me the pimp picked her up in that car?" she asked, holding up the phone.

Mark nodded, looking relieved that she seemed to believe him. "Yeah. That's his car. I never saw her again."

Rachel stared as the video played out. The car drove away in a cloud of dust, taking the victim with it.

And Mark remained behind, holding the camera and uttering a string of colorful obscenities at his mid-coital interruption.

Rachel checked the timestamp on the video.

The same night the woman would've died judging from initial medical reports. Mark wasn't the killer.

"What's the name of that pimp?" she said firmly.

He just shrugged at her. "Dunno. Never got it."

Rachel let out a long breath. "I'm going to check this video," she said.

"Fine. Do it. It's real."

"It better be," she murmured, and then she turned and hastened to the door.

If he was telling the truth, then the last person to see their victim alive likely was the muscled man with the tattoos.

So now… the question was how to lure a pimp out of hiding.

CHAPTER EIGHTEEN

The full moon cast a silvery glow over the vast expanse of desert, a landscape dotted with cacti and rocky outcroppings. The wind whispered through the night, stirring up a fine mist of sand that danced around their feet. It was midnight, and there, in the heart of this desolate domain, stood the man, his tall figure looming over his captive.

Her wrists chafed against the rough rope binding her to the trunk of a twisted Joshua tree. Her eyes darted back and forth, searching for any avenue of escape.

"Please," she whispered, her voice barely audible above the wind.

The man looked down at her, his cold eyes showing neither sympathy nor malice. His voice, when he finally spoke, was calm and collected, like a snake slithering through the underbrush. "This is not your fault," he said softly. "But it must be done."

"Who are you?" she demanded, struggling to keep her voice steady. "What do you want from me?"

"Shh," the killer soothed, his tone almost gentle. He could feel the bitter tang of sadness as he watched her. She didn't deserve this. But it would all end eventually. "Soon, you'll understand."

His gaze shifted from his captive to the vast, dark sky above them. He seemed almost hypnotized by the inky expanse, as if he were waiting for something. The desert air hung heavy with the scent of imminent rain, and far off in the distance, the faint rumble of thunder resonated through the desolate landscape.

"The rain is coming," he said, a small smile playing on his lips. "It will be here soon."

"Wh-what happens when it rains?" she asked, her voice tremulous.

"Ah, the rain," he murmured. "It brings life, doesn't it? And yet, it can also wash away the old, making way for the new."

"Please, if you have any humanity left in you, let me go," she whispered, her voice barely audible above the steadily increasing wind. "I-I promise I won't tell anyone about this."

The man merely shook his head, his eyes never leaving the stormy sky. "I'm afraid that's not possible," he replied, and he could tell his words chilled her to the core. “You see, some things are simply meant to be washed away. Most people underestimate the power of the rain,” the man mused, as he drew a large hunting knife from a sheath. He ignored the woman’s question, instead focusing on the sharp blade in his hands. With a practiced motion, he began to sharpen it against a rock, his eyes never leaving her face.

The rhythmic sound of metal scraping against stone caused her to flinch with every stroke.

His face remained impassive, betraying no hint of emotion.

“Rain has a way of purging the earth, you know,” he said softly, his voice barely audible above the wind that had begun to howl around them. “It washes away the sins of the past, leaving only purity behind.”

She whimpered, but it was as if he heard words. As if he thought she’d asked him a question, though she hadn’t said a word.

He tilted his head briefly.

“Imagined?” he whispered. “I assure you, my dear, our sins are all too real. And soon, the rain will come, and we shall both be cleansed.”

As he continued to methodically sharpen the knife, the clouds rolled in, dark across the sky.

Time was running out.

CHAPTER NINETEEN

Rachel leaned against the cold brick wall, her breath forming a misty cloud in the crisp night air. It often surprised people how chilly it could get near the desert. The moon cast a silvery glow over the narrow alleyway, casting long shadows that seemed to dance and sway with each gust of wind. She glanced at Ethan, who stood a few feet away from her, his tall frame hunched as he kept watch for any sign of the tattooed pimp they'd been tracking. They both wore plain clothes, blending seamlessly into the dark corners of the city.

They'd been waiting for the last few hours after placing the call through the website.

And now, Rachel was finding it difficult to keep her mind occupied.

As she stood there, inhaling the musty scent of the dank alley, her thoughts drifted to the conversation she had with Aunt Sarah. Her aunt's words still echoed in her mind, bringing up painful memories of her parents' unsolved murders. Rachel clenched her fists, her nails digging into her palms. No, she couldn't afford to be distracted now. She had to focus on the case at hand.

"Help me set this up," Rachel whispered to Ethan, motioning to a thin string and some empty cans she'd gathered. Together, they rigged the makeshift alarm system—a bush trap Sarah had once taught her—in the mouth of the alley. If their target walked into the string, the cans would tumble, alerting them to his presence. Rachel would have to stay out of sight, so the sound of the cans would alert her to come to Ethan's aid.

Ethan was playing the john.

With the trap in place, Rachel slunk back toward the large, graffiti-covered dumpster, its foul stench making her nose wrinkle.

The alley was littered with the detritus of urban life—broken bottles, discarded newspapers, and the occasional rat scurrying across the cracked pavement. A single flickering streetlamp struggled to illuminate the space, creating an eerie atmosphere that sent shivers down Rachel's spine.

"Remember, we need him alive," Rachel murmured to Ethan, her eyes scanning the entrance of the alley for any sign of movement.

"I… that wasn't even a consideration," Ethan replied. He tensed. "You don't think we'll have to shoot, do you?"

"No. You should be fine."

"Thanks. Thanks, I feel very reassured."

She nodded once and her fingers tightened around the handle of her gun, the metal cool and reassuring in her grip. She lowered the brim of her hat to prevent it from sticking up and over the dumpster where she hid. Two wooden pallets also obscured her view of the mouth of the alley.

Ethan lingered under the fire escape, also out of sight. They needed the pimp to come further into the alley. Closer to them, so he couldn't escape.

But this also meant they couldn't keep eyes on the entrance.

The can trick would work.

They would just have to be patient.

Together, they waited in the shadows, anticipation building with each passing second.

She studied her partner, where he stood in the middle of the alley, a few paces ahead of her. His posture was casual, but Rachel could see the tension radiating from him. She found she liked watching him. He had a confidence that belied his sometimes overly eager disposition.

Suddenly, he tensed.

The cans made a rattling sound.

There was a soft mutter. A curse.

Rachel felt a surge of adrenaline course through her veins. This could be it.

She risked a glance around the edge of the pallets, emerging slightly; if she spooked them, it would all be over.

A man stepped forward, followed by a woman from the passenger side. As they came into the light, Rachel's heart sank. The man had no tattoos, nor did he resemble the pimp they were pursuing. She hesitated for a moment, considering their options. But something about the man's demeanor set off alarm bells in her head.

He kept glancing around, scowling and rubbing at his wrists.

"Damn it," she muttered under her breath, making a split-second decision. Rachel emerged from her hiding place, gun drawn and aimed at the man. "Don't move! Hands where I can see them!"

The man froze, his face a mixture of shock and terror. The woman let out a yelp, her eyes darting between Rachel and Ethan.

“Whoa, whoa! We ain’t done nothing wrong!” the man protested, lifting his hands in surrender.

“Keep your hands up,” Ethan snapped, joining Rachel with his own gun drawn. He looked at Rachel, his eyes questioning their next move. This hadn’t been the plan. But he could clearly see the man didn’t match the pimp they were pursuing. Something was off.

The man who’d come wore a neat suit and a tie-dye headband. His face was roughly shaven, with a few scars marring his jawline. He was tall and muscular, with a presence that demanded attention. His eyes were a piercing blue, and Rachel could see the anger burning in them.

“Who are you?” Rachel demanded, keeping her eyes trained on the man.

“I could ask you the same thing,” the man replied, his voice low and gravelly.

“Texas Rangers,” Ethan interjected, taking a step forward. “Who are you?”

“Who you expecting?” he said, his eyes glancing slyly back and forth. He kept his hands raised, though, his posture cautious. “Me and my girlfriend here,” he said, nodding at the woman trembling against the wall, her mascara streaking. “We just going for a walk is all, see?”

“Of course,” Ethan snapped.

“Can we keep goin’? Not nice accosting a couple’a citizens.”

Rachel glanced at her phone with the screenshot of the pimp who’d driven off with Candy, their third victim.

This man definitely wasn’t a match.

Rachel felt her heart sink. They’d wasted precious time on a dead end. But something about the man’s demeanor made her uneasy.

“Can we see some ID?” she asked, keeping her gun trained on him.

The man hesitated for a moment, then reached slowly into his pocket and pulled out a wallet. Rachel motioned for him to toss it to her, and he complied. She caught it with her free hand and flipped it open, scanning the ID.

“Michael Thompson,” she read aloud, her brow furrowing. “You’re a long way from home, aren’t you, Mr. Thompson?”

The man shrugged, his eyes still flickering with anger. “I travel a lot for work.”

“What kind of work?”

“Consulting.”

Rachel locked her gaze on the man, trying to read his intentions. "We're looking for someone," she said, voice steady and authoritative. "And you're not the person we called."

He blinked. "You called?"

"Yeah, that was us," Ethan said.

"I don't know anything about no call."

The woman was shaking her head in agreement.

"You sure you want to play it like that?" Rachel asked.

Ethan said, "We got a line on your phone, you know. Y'all playing games."

Rachel had noticed Ethan's southern accent became more pronounced when he was agitated. The handsome man's sharp features seemed to aim in one direction as he jutted his chin at the pimp.

"You sayin' you got my phone?" the man said. He bit his lip.

"We're not looking for you," Rachel cut in. "We don't have any business with you. We're looking for your colleague."

"Oh…" He trailed off, frowning as if deep in consideration. It looked painful. "Who?"

"A pimp with tattoos working this area."

"Look, lady, I don't know what you're talking about," the man stammered, sweat beading on his forehead. "We're just here for some… night out."

"Then you won't mind us checking that out, will you?" Rachel asked, her eyes narrowing. "Take you downtown with us. Have a look into your background. Hopefully, you don't have any priors. Or, God forbid, an arrest warrant."

Suddenly, the woman bolted. She let out a little yelp and took off. Her high heels lay abandoned on the cold alley ground.

Ethan glanced sharply at Rachel, but she shook her head. She considered giving chase, but her gut told her they needed answers from the man in front of them more than they needed to pursue the woman. "Let her go," she said tersely, her focus returning to the apprehended pimp.

Ethan nodded, his grip on his gun unwavering as he continued to cover their suspect.

"Look," the man said, glancing over his shoulder and scowling as he seemed to realize he was now on his own. "I… I don't know what I can tell you. We don't have to take this downtown though. We can chat." Now that the witness was gone, he seemed more willing to talk.

"Alright," Rachel said, her deep brown eyes boring into the man as she holstered her weapon. "You're going to tell us everything you know about the pimp with tattoos working this area. And don't even think about lying to me."

The man hesitated for a moment, fear glittering in his eyes as he weighed his options. "I've seen him around," he admitted finally, his voice shaky. "He goes by the name Snake. We all know him. I just took over for him yesterday."

"Where can we find him?" Ethan interjected, his tone demanding.

"Look, I don't know, okay?" the man replied, desperation creeping into his voice. "I just see him sometimes when I'm here for… other business."

Rachel clenched her teeth, the frustration mounting within her.

"You just lied to me," Rachel said softly.

He stared at her.

She was guessing, but his reaction confirmed it.

"I…"

"Where's Snake?" she demanded. "Or we do this downtown."

"Shit, man. You should know. He's gonezo. Donezo. You know?" The man's words hung heavy in the air, a palpable tension settling over the alley. "Snake was shot and killed a couple nights ago," he mumbled, avoiding Rachel's gaze.

Ethan and Rachel went quiet.

"Is that so?" she asked skeptically, her voice cold as ice. She glanced at Ethan, who looked stunned.

"Why not call it in, then, man!" he exclaimed. "Come on—I'm not lying!"

Ethan had already pulled his phone out. He placed it on speaker and gave a significant glance toward their suspect. But Rachel felt a slow, creeping sense of unease.

The man didn't look nervous now. As if he knew his story would check out.

"Officer Daniels speaking," came the voice on the other end.

"Ethan Morgan, Texas Rangers," he replied curtly. "I need to confirm an alleged death—a pimp known as Snake."

"Give me a moment, I'll check our records," Officer Daniels said, the faint sound of keyboard clicks filtering through the call.

As Rachel waited, her heart pounded in her chest. She couldn't shake the feeling that this lead was slipping away, much like the others before it.

"Morgan?" Officer Daniels's voice brought her back to the present. "I can confirm that a man fitting Snake's description was found dead two nights ago. Shot multiple times."

"Thank you, Officer Daniels," Ethan said, disconnecting the call. He stared at his phone for a moment, the screen's glow reflecting in his deep brown eyes. Then he looked up, wincing at her.

"So our killer took out the pimp… and then attacked Candy."

"Candy?" their suspect repeated. "Holy shit. She's dead?"

Rachel didn't reply. The frustration grew inside her, gnawing relentlessly at her resolve.

"Can I… can I go?" he pressed.

She stared at him. There was no reason to keep him. Nothing tying him to the murder.

So she shrugged.

He began inching away. When no one moved to stop him, he spun on his heel and sprinted.

"Dead end," she muttered. "Literally." She locked eyes with Ethan, searching for any hint of a plan in his expression. "What do we do now?"

"Let's focus on the first victim—the heiress billionaire," Ethan suggested, his voice steady and calm. "We might find something we missed before."

Rachel nodded, the gears in her mind already shifting to this new course of action. It wasn't ideal, but it was a path forward, and she couldn't afford to waste any more time on dead ends.

As they walked down the dimly lit street, the shadows of the buildings growing longer in the fading light, Rachel's thoughts turned to the wealthy billionaire. She remembered the details of her life—the lavish parties, the jet-setting lifestyle, the trail of broken relationships she left behind.

Broken relationships were often the first stone to look under.

Was she making this more complicated than necessary? Allowing the whistles and bells to distract her from the obvious?

"Her ex-husband," Rachel said suddenly, stopping in her tracks as the idea took hold. "He's local. We need to talk to him."

Ethan raised an eyebrow, the skepticism clear on his face. "You think he'll actually talk to us? He's a powerful man, and from what I've heard, not exactly eager to discuss his past."

Rachel's jaw set, her gaze unwavering. "He might know something that could help us find the killer. We have to try."

“Alright,” Ethan conceded, his tone cautious. “But getting an audience with him won’t be easy. He’s known for being reclusive, and he’s got layers of security around him.”

“Then we’ll find a way through those layers,” Rachel declared, her voice firm and resolute. The memory of her aunt’s lessons flickered through her mind, reminding her of the importance of persistence and resourcefulness.

The two of them approached their parked car, moving quickly now.

CHAPTER TWENTY

The next morning, the sun cast an orange glow over the sprawling oil estate as Rachel and Ethan pulled up to the imposing gates. It was a Texas-sized fortress, complete with manicured lawns, a glistening fountain, and rows of towering palm trees lining the driveway. The name "Grayson Jefferson" hung in gold lettering above the entrance, leaving no doubt about the wealth and status of the man who resided within these walls.

"Looks like he's doing well for himself," Ethan muttered, his gaze narrowing as they assessed the property.

"Too well, maybe," Rachel replied, her deep brown eyes filled with determination.

As they approached the front door, it swung open to reveal Grayson Jefferson himself: tall, impeccably groomed, and radiating an air of cold detachment. He had silver hair and features that weren't nearly as wrinkled as the birthdate on his DMV photo would've suggested. He wore expensive, designer clothing with the logos proudly displayed, and there was an imperious tilt to his chin.

It had taken them five phone calls, three favors, and a dozen threats to get this meeting.

He didn't offer them a smile or any sign of warmth, and Rachel could feel the tension in the air thicken as he regarded them with icy green eyes.

"Ranger Blackwood, I presume?" he drawled, barely acknowledging Ethan's presence. "I suppose you're here to ask me questions about my ex-wife's murder?"

Straight and to the point. A man used to being in charge and in control.

She came to a stop at the bottom of the marble steps, one hand trailing against an ornate, curling, lacquered railing.

"Yes, Mr. Jefferson," Rachel said, forcing herself to maintain eye contact despite the chill she felt from his demeanor.

"Fine," he sighed, stepping aside to let them in. "But make it quick. I'm a busy man."

As they followed him into the opulent foyer, Rachel couldn't help but notice the extravagance surrounding them. Marble floors, crystal chandeliers, and priceless works of art adorned every corner of the room. It was a stark contrast to the humble home she had shared with Sarah.

"Have a seat." Grayson gestured toward a lavish sitting area, his voice devoid of any warmth. Somehow, he made this sound like a command rather than an offer. "What do you want to know?"

They both settled slowly. Rachel's chair was uncomfortable.

"Mr. Jefferson, can you tell us about your ex-wife?" Rachel asked, her deep brown eyes unyielding as they met Grayson's icy gaze.

Grayson leaned back in his leather armchair, his face a mask of indifference. "What do you want to know?" he repeated, his words clipped.

"We're investigating her murder, Mr. Jefferson," Rachel replied calmly. "We need to know everything you can tell us about her."

Grayson sighed and ran a hand through his perfectly styled hair. "Beau was a complicated woman," he said finally. "Smart, beautiful, but troubled. She had a lot of demons."

"What kind of demons?" Ethan interjected, his voice low and steady.

Grayson gave him a withering look. "The kind that come from a difficult past," he spat. "She had a rough childhood, and it affected her deeply. She struggled with addiction, with depression, with trust issues."

"And how did you fit into all of this?" Rachel asked, her voice even.

Grayson's eyes flickered with something unreadable. "I tried to help her," he said slowly. "But she was a difficult person to help. She didn't like to be told what to do, and she didn't like to be beholden to anyone."

Rachel leaned forward, her gaze intent on Grayson's face. "Did you ever hurt her, Mr. Jefferson?" she asked quietly.

Grayson's eyes narrowed. "What kind of question is that?" he snapped. "Of course not. I loved Madison. I would never hurt her."

Rachel didn't back down. "There are reports that she filed a restraining order against you," she said. "Can you explain that?"

Grayson's face twisted in anger. "That was a misunderstanding. She was going through an episode."

Grayson shifted in his plush armchair, clearly uncomfortable under the weight of her scrutiny.

"What sort of episode?"

He waved dismissively. "Some political rally fell through."

Rachel perked up. "Your ex was into politics?"

"She donated to a few campaigns, but nothing out of the ordinary," he replied, his voice tight with impatience. "I don't see how that could possibly be related to her murder."

"Did she ever mention any concerns or threats from these politicians? Or perhaps someone who was unhappy with her support?" Ethan interjected, leaning forward and resting his elbows on his knees.

"No," Grayson snapped, his cold demeanor beginning to crack under their relentless questioning. "And even if she did, we were no longer married. She had her own life, and I had mine."

Rachel studied his face for any hint of deception, her thoughts racing as she considered their next move.

"Is there anyone else we should be aware of who might have had a motive to harm your ex-wife?" Rachel pressed, her determination to find answers shining through her unwavering gaze.

"Look, I've told you all I know," Grayson said tersely, crossing his arms over his chest. "I didn't have anything to do with her death." His eyes darted to the ornate grandfather clock that stood against the far wall. "Now if you don't mind, I have an important call to make."

She thought of the victims. Her mind on Harley Reid, whose identity was just confirmed. On the others. She frowned.

"Do you know the name Harley Reid?" Rachel said before he could separate himself from the situation, her mind racing through a mental checklist of questions as she studied the wealthy oil baron's face for any flicker of recognition.

He shook his head. "Who's that?"

"What about Candy?"

"Just... *Candy*?"

"Yes."

"No. Why?"

"Two other bodies were found buried near where your ex was discovered."

He blinked, looking temporarily taken aback.

Now that the ID had come in on both of the new victims, Rachel still couldn't find the pattern. Neither of the two other bodies belonged to anyone wealthy or connected. So what was going on here?

"Harley Reid was the waitress we found near your ex-wife's body. Did you or your ex-wife know her? Any connection at all?"

Grayson's eyebrows furrowed, his eyes searching hers for a moment before he shook his head. "I have never heard of that girl," he said firmly. "As far as I know, neither did my ex-wife."

"Who would have access to the oil fields where we found their bodies?" Rachel asked, her voice like steel. "Specifically, who has the clearance to bypass security measures there?"

"Only a select few have that kind of access," Grayson admitted, a hint of annoyance creeping into his voice. "Myself, my head of security, and a few trusted employees. Why are you asking?"

"Because someone with access must have been involved in hiding the bodies," Ethan interjected, his piercing gaze fixed on Grayson.

"Or perhaps they simply knew how to avoid detection," Rachel added, her thoughts whirring as she considered the implications of this information. "Do you have any reason to suspect any of them, Mr. Jefferson?"

"Of course not," he snapped, his eyes dark with anger. "My people are loyal to me, and I trust them completely."

"Then we'll need their names and contact information," Rachel said quietly, her mind already assembling a list of potential leads to pursue.

"Fine," Grayson muttered, pulling out his phone to send the details to them. "But I assure you, none of them had anything to do with this."

Rachel studied Grayson Jefferson's face, searching for any flicker of recognition or guilt. But his countenance remained a carefully constructed mask, impenetrable and cold. He shifted in his seat, still looking down at his phone.

"Security cameras cover all known entrances to the oil fields," Grayson said, his tone dismissive. "We have extensive footage, but I doubt you'll find anything of value there."

"Footage?" Ethan said, alert all of a sudden.

"Let us be the judge of that, Mr. Jefferson," Rachel said, her voice firm. "We'd like to see the footage ourselves."

"Very well," he conceded with a sigh. "I'll have someone bring it up."

Ethan leaned back in his chair, his eyes never straying from Grayson. The tension in the room was palpable, every tick of the grandfather clock echoing through the vast sitting room like a drumbeat. Rachel couldn't help but notice the opulence surrounding them—the gold-framed paintings, the crystal decanters, the thick

Persian rugs—and she wondered how many secrets lay hidden within these gilded walls.

Grayson just glared right back at her as if he were issuing a challenge, refusing to be intimidated.

Rachel didn't really care.

She'd stared down grizzly bears before.

She'd hunted thousand-pound monsters.

Eventually, every predator had a crack—a weakness to exploit.

She just had to find it. And the security footage might be the best lead they had.

CHAPTER TWENTY ONE

"Here we are," a young assistant announced as he entered the sitting room where the three of them waited in cold, stony silence. The assistant was holding a laptop. He placed it on the coffee table before them, and Rachel couldn't help but notice the tremble in his hands. "The footage is organized by date and time."

"Thank you," Rachel murmured, opening the screen.

She could feel Jefferson watching her. Could feel Ethan shifting side to side behind her where he paced on the Persian rug.

She focused on the screen, though, refusing distraction.

"Login details?" she muttered.

Jefferson just said, "Pass123."

"Nice," Ethan replied.

Rachel just entered the information, her fingers flying across the keyboard as she navigated through the footage files.

"Start with the days leading up to the discovery of the bodies," Ethan suggested, his focus locked on the screen.

Rachel nodded, her eyes scanning the files. She found the ones she needed and clicked on the first video. The footage was grainy, but she could make out the gate in the darkness.

"Nothing," Rachel said. She tapped the arrow keys, cycling through the footage.

Both of them could feel their unwilling host growing more and more irritated with them.

But Rachel didn't look in Grayson's direction, preferring to keep her eyes glued to the screen.

"Wait," Ethan whispered suddenly, freezing a frame on the screen. "Go back a few seconds."

Rachel complied, rewinding the footage to reveal a figure approaching one of the entrances. As they watched, the shadowy form slipped into the darkness beyond the camera's reach, vanishing into the night.

"Who is that?" Rachel asked, her pulse quickening.

"Hard to say," Ethan admitted, his brow furrowed in concentration.

They paused the footage, trying to make out the figure moving in the dark.

Grayson leaned in, frowning. “That’s odd,” he said.

“What?”

“The time. No one should have been onsite at two a.m.”

Rachel glanced in the corner of the footage toward the small, blinking digital clock.

She felt her pulse skip a beat. Her gaze returned to the grainy figure moving in the muddy terrain.

She hesitated, spotting something in the mud.

Rachel squinted at the security footage on the computer screen, her deep brown eyes scanning. Her worn Stetson sat atop her jet-black hair, and the beads she’d woven into a braid clinked softly as she leaned in closer. The hum of the overhead light was barely audible over the faint whirring of the computer fan.

“Right there,” she muttered to herself. “Tire treads. Those weren’t there at the start of the footage.”

She cycled back a bit more.

“Stop!” Ethan said suddenly.

She’d already hit the spacebar.

Both of them watched as, for a split second, a red sedan entered the frame. Suddenly, the vehicle reversed and sped away from the scene, tires screeching against the mud. A few moments later, the dark, hooded figure had appeared. “Strange…” Rachel’s brow furrowed as she replayed the clip several times, committing every detail to memory.

“Got the tag?”

“I saw ’em. Yeah,” she said, nodding at Ethan. “Let me run the plates real quick.” She typed the numbers into the database, her fingers deftly dancing across the keyboard.

Within moments, the search results appeared on the screen. “Jeremiah Smith,” Rachel read aloud, her eyes narrowing. “A driver for an oil barrel company. The car was reported stolen last week.”

“Stolen?” her partner echoed, rubbing his chin thoughtfully. “You think he might be our guy?”

“Could be,” Rachel mused, clicking through Smith’s profile. She did a quick web search.

Rachel’s eyes flicked back to Jeremiah Smith’s profile on the computer screen, her brow furrowing in thought. She noticed a string of posts he had made on social media. She clicked on these, from a few months ago, following the link.

“Hey,” she said, pointing at the screen for her partner to see. “Look at this. Our Mr. Smith appears to have quite the political chip on his shoulder.”

“Interesting,” Ethan murmured, leaning in to read the posts. “Wasn’t our first victim involved in political contributions?”

Grayson was standing by the window now, and his shoulders tensed at this comment, but he didn’t glance back at them.

“Could be,” Rachel mused, her fingers tracing the edge of her jacket. The leather was cool beneath her touch.

“Seems like it’s worth checking out,” her partner agreed, straightening up and looking at her expectantly. “Shall we pay him a visit?”

“Let’s find out if his politics align with our case.”

CHAPTER TWENTY TWO

The sun hung low in the sky, casting long shadows across the dusty exterior of the mechanic's shop. Rachel squinted against the glare, her deep brown eyes narrowing as she and Ethan approached the entrance. Her hair was pulled back into a tight braid now, kept out of her face.

"Jeremiah Smith?" Ethan called out as he knocked on the door, his voice echoing through the desolate area. Rachel pushed the door open, revealing the dimly lit interior of the shop, cluttered with tools and machinery. The smell of oil and gasoline filled their nostrils, a familiar scent for those who lived in this part of Texas. They stepped inside cautiously, eyes scanning the space for any signs of life.

"Hello?" Rachel shouted, her voice steady and authoritative. "We just want to talk."

Silence greeted them, broken only by the distant sound of a wrench clattering to the floor. Rachel exchanged a knowing glance with Ethan before they both moved further into the shop.

"Must be someone here," Ethan muttered, his eyes darting around the room.

As if in response, an old, nervous man emerged from behind a stack of tires, his skin greasy and stained from years of labor. His hands trembled slightly, betraying his unease. "Hey there, strangers."

"Rangers," Rachel said quickly, raising her badge with practiced ease.

He didn't look surprised. "Mhmm," the old-timer said, nodding and adjusting his coveralls with a hooked thumb. "Who are you looking for?" he asked, attempting to feign ignorance. "I don't know anyone named Jeremiah."

"Now which is it? You wondering who we're looking for? Or you don't know anyone named Jeremiah?" Rachel said.

He looked flustered and paused briefly. His words had come fast and jumbled at first, but now he just looked uncertain.

Rachel could sense the dishonesty in his voice, her instincts honed from years spent tracking people through the Texas wilderness. She locked her gaze on him. "We heard something in the back."

Just then, the faint sound of shuffling reached their ears, followed by a creaking. Rachel and Ethan exchanged another glance before they both sprang into action, brushing past the old-timer and hurrying in the direction of the noise. It sounded like a window being forced open.

"You can't go back there!" the old-timer protested.

"Watch us," Rachel retorted.

They pushed through a door that led into one of the work areas. The place smelled even more strongly of grease. But Rachel's gaze was drawn to a figure in the back.

"Stop!" Ethan shouted as they both caught sight of a man struggling to slip through a rear-facing window.

Rachel bolted like a runner at a starter pistol, leaping over a bench covered in oily rags and lunging toward the man who was huffing and cursing as he struggled through the small window.

Rachel's lithe, athletic build allowed her to close the distance quickly, her strong legs propelling her forward like a predator chasing its prey. She lunged for the man, fingertips brushing against his clothing, but he slipped through her grasp, disappearing out the window. Cursing under her breath, she pushed herself up from the ground, her determination undeterred.

The roar of an engine starting in the alleyway alerted them to the escaping man's plan.

Without a moment's hesitation, Rachel and Ethan sprinted back to their car.

"Stop, hang on!" the old-timer called.

But they both ignored his stall tactics as they flung themselves through the door and back to their waiting car. A moment later, they peeled out of the mechanic's shop, tires screeching against the pavement. In hot pursuit of the fleeing man, they tore onto the desolate desert roads that stretched endlessly across the Texas landscape.

"Stay on him!" Rachel shouted, her deep brown eyes fixated on the cloud of dust kicked up by the other vehicle.

Ethan gripped the wheel tightly while his foot pressed down hard on the gas pedal. Their car sped through the barren landscape, catching up to the fleeing driver who was now veering off-road. A cloud of sand billowed behind them as both vehicles tore across the rugged terrain.

"Rachel, you ready?" Ethan asked, glancing over at her.

She just nodded once and braced herself.

Ethan swung the car wide, slamming the front bumper into the rear of the other car.

The other vehicle spun out on the sandy, off-road terrain. It struck a divot, and there was a screech of metal.

The car went suddenly still.

"You good?" Ethan asked, breathing heavily as they came to a rolling stop behind their prey.

In answer, Rachel leapt out onto the sandy ground.

"Turn off your engine!" Rachel commanded, her authoritative tone cutting through the air like a knife.

She strode toward the stalled car in the ditch. The man complied, his hands shaking as he raised them in surrender out the window.

At least he was still conscious.

As Rachel approached the defeated driver, she got a good look at him. Jeremiah Smith—his features matched the DMV photo she had on her phone. She compared the two for a moment, then turned her attention to the real deal.

He seemed genuinely terrified, his face pale and streaked with sweat.

"What the hell!" he yelled at her. "What was that for?"

"You ran," she said simply.

He bit his lip and grimaced as if it hurt.

She peered into the car. "Are you alright?"

"No!" he retorted. "You ran me off the damn road!"

She glanced back, then at him once more. "Actually, you went off the road. We just helped you into the ditch."

He glared at her, but as she scanned him, he seemed unharmed, so she leaned back, hand resting on her weapon at her hip.

She tapped the top of his car. "You reported a stolen vehicle. Same make as this one—different color."

He didn't reply, but just scowled at her.

She waved a hand in front of her face to clear the dust drifting around them. Ethan was behind her, watching closely but not volunteering any information.

"My car?"

He rubbed at his forehead, sweaty, his hands still raised. He swallowed as he nervously glanced at her weapon. "This is about my damn car?"

She considered arresting him, taking him back to a precinct, and interrogating him there. But now… he seemed so flustered. Off guard.

This was the perfect time for answers.

"Your car was at the oil fields," she began, her voice firm yet measured. "I don't think it was stolen."

"The… wait, what? Oil fields? Y-you're wrong!" the man stammered, his eyes darting from side to side as if searching for an escape route.

"I think you're lying to me," Rachel said. "I think you know who was in that car. "Was it you?"

He just looked shell-shocked and kept shaking his head.

"Really?" Ethan chimed in, pointing at the wheel well on the man's car. "You painted over it recently."

Rachel glanced back, impressed at Ethan's sharp eye. She noted the faint tinge of double color at the edge of the wheel well. She turned her attention back to Jeremiah.

"You're still driving the car you reported stolen." She didn't phrase it as a question.

"What? No! No, of course not."

"Cut it out," Rachel said simply. "You're on a murder rap. Lying isn't going to help you."

At the word *murder*, he went still. The mechanic had oversized eyes and an expression that made him seem constantly surprised.

"You were at the oil fields," she said quietly. "We can run the tire treads. Your tires haven't been changed in a while."

She levied each word like a scalpel to peel away more layers of denial.

The man looked stunned, as if he'd been slapped. Panic washed over his face, and he began to break down, shaking his head, stuttering, "I didn't know!"

"Didn't know what?"

"About any of it. I… I was just dropping something off. Burying it."

"Bullshit."

"I was!"

"Bullshit," she repeated.

"I didn't know what it was till I got there."

"You didn't know what *what* was?"

"The bodies," he said, staring at her with a panicked look in his eyes.

Ethan tensed.

Her own hand tightened around the grip of the weapon.

"What do you mean?" she said sharply. "The bodies were in your car?"

"I didn't know! I swear it. I didn't. I swear on—on my own mother!"

She frowned at the man. He looked sick, the blood having left his face. "So you admit you had the bodies in the trunk of your car?"

He swallowed, glancing nervously from her to Ethan and back again.

"I was paid in cash. That's all I know."

"Who put you up to it?" Rachel demanded, her gaze locked onto the panicked man. "Tell us everything you know."

"I-I can't," he stammered, his fear palpable. "Please, just let me go."

Rachel's glare bored into the man, her dark eyes unrelenting. She could sense his fear.

"Start with what you did," she said, her tone ice-cold.

"Alright, alright," he stammered, taking a deep breath. "I buried something out in the oil fields."

"Buried what?" Ethan asked, crossing his arms over his chest.

"I didn't know! I swear!" the man insisted, shaking his head frantically.

"Who told you to bury them?" she pressed, her voice like steel.

"I don't know," the man whispered, his gaze fixed on the dusty ground as he peered through his stalled vehicle's open window.

"Tell us exactly what happened," Rachel demanded, her mind racing as she tried to piece together the puzzle before her.

"Okay, okay," he said, wiping the sweat from his brow. "Some guy came to the shop a few weeks ago. He offered me a lot of money if I'd bury some things for him out in the oil fields. He never told me what they were, just gave me the coordinates and said it had to be done at night. I didn't ask questions. I just needed the money."

Rachel clenched her fists, struggling to control her anger. Was he lying? He seemed genuine. But sociopaths could play the game when cornered.

"What did the man look like?"

"No clue."

"I thought you said you met him."

"He was in his car. Windows tinted, rolled up. We spoke through the glass."

"What was the car like?"

"Buick. Engine modded."

"License plate?"

He shook his head. "None. Temporary he said, but it was completely missing. Besides… after he told me what he wanted, I assumed he didn't want anyone to know."

"Where did he find you? How did he know you were desperate enough to do this?" Rachel asked, trying to find any possible connection. But what if he was lying? It came down to that as well, didn't it?

"I-I don't know!" the man exclaimed. "I never even met him before he approached me. I hang around the garage sometimes, maybe he saw me there?"

Under the merciless Texas sun, Rachel leaned against the hood of the car, arms crossed over her chest as she fixed a steely gaze on the driver. Sweat trickled down her temple as she adjusted her hat to shield her eyes. She could feel the heat radiating from the sun, but she refused to let it break her composure.

"Listen," she said in a low, unyielding tone. "You've already admitted to helping bury something out in the oil fields. You say you didn't know what it was, but that doesn't change the fact that you were involved. So give me one damn good reason not to think you killed them and are coming up with some bullshit story."

"I'm not!"

"Prove it!"

"How?"

Rachel hesitated. The victims had all been drowned. In oil. But what if… what if *not* the oil fields? What if Jeremiah was telling the truth? He'd been given bodies in bags, or something similar, and then dropped them into the oil pits. Perhaps even in soluble sheeting that dissolved after a few hours.

But on the other hand… what if he was just bullshitting?

"Where were you Thursday night?" she said finally.

The night their first victim had gone missing.

"I… umm…" Suddenly his eyes widened. The driver's eyes darted between Rachel and Ethan, his hands wringing together nervously. He swallowed hard. "At a club! I was at a club. And… I can prove it!"

His hand moved sharply.

"Watch it!" Ethan yelled.

Jeremiah squeaked, going still. "Just… just reaching for my phone," he stammered.

"Slowly," Ethan growled.

Jeremiah nodded quickly, moving his hand cautiously toward his pocket now, with much slower motions.

He pulled out his phone. "I was there from eight until two a.m.," he said, excitedly.

He turned the phone, and Rachel scanned through the pictures with time stamps. She frowned as her finger flicked along the screen.

"Well?" Ethan said.

She hesitated, double-checking there were no gaps in the timeframe wide enough for him to have slipped away. But there weren't. The pictures were completely indecent, but she didn't focus on the content nearly as much as the time frame.

He hadn't been involved in the heiress's disappearance. Which meant… he was either telling the truth, or he had an accomplice.

She looked at the man, at his sputtering, terrified disposition.

He wasn't a killer. She didn't think so, at least. She had a scent for predators. How easy had it been to get him to confess?

No… he wasn't smart enough to pull this off.

He was driving the same car he'd reported stolen, but had just repainted it.

"I believe you," she said simply.

He looked at her wide-eyed.

"You're just dumb enough for me to believe you," she said, nodding pensively.

He frowned a bit.

Before she could press further, Rachel's phone vibrated in her pocket. She pulled it out.

"Hello?" she asked tentatively.

"Ranger Blackwood?" came a voice from the other end, urgently. "This is Deputy O'Connor. We've just found another body. It's fresh."

"Where?" Rachel demanded, her senses immediately sharpening.

"Different oil field than the last ones. About fifty miles north. I'll send co-ords," Deputy O'Connor replied, his voice tense. "You and Ranger Morgan need to get here as soon as possible."

"Understood. We're on our way," Rachel said, hanging up the phone.

"New crime scene?" Ethan asked, already fishing cuffs from his pocket to arrest their suspect.

"Fresh body," Rachel confirmed, her mind racing with possibilities. They needed to move fast.

CHAPTER TWENTY THREE

In between gathering clouds, the moon gleamed in the sky, casting faultless shadows across the dusty field as Rachel pulled the truck to a stop. The crime scene lay before her: an unsettling tableau framed by the gathering crowd from the nearby oil town. She stepped out of the vehicle, her leather boots crunching on the parched earth beneath her.

"Alright, folks, stand back," she called out, scanning the sea of faces, worn and weary from a life spent under the relentless Texas sun. There were about thirty people present, a mix of men and women, ranging in age from early twenties to late sixties. Most of them wore grease-stained clothes that bore testament to their laborious existence; a few sported hats adorned with the insignias of local oil companies.

Rachel could sense their collective anxiety; it emanated from them like heat off a car hood. They fidgeted and whispered amongst themselves, craning their necks for a better look at the grim spectacle. It wasn't every day that death came calling in such an intimate way.

"Please, give us some space to work," she implored, adjusting her hat to shield her deep brown eyes from the glare of the moon. She noticed the clouds were thickening.

Ethan stepped out behind her, indicated by the thud of the passenger side door. He followed quietly in her wake.

As she led him toward the crime scene, she couldn't help but feel a pang of sympathy for these townsfolk—they were strangers to the brutality she had witnessed all too often in her line of work. But this was no time for sentimentality; there was a victim lying cold in the dirt, waiting for answers that only she could provide.

"Lord have mercy," muttered an elderly woman, making the sign of the cross as Rachel strode past.

"Alright, folks," Rachel called out, trying to maintain an air of authority as she approached the restless crowd. "I need you all to clear the area so we can properly contain this crime scene."

A burly man with a graying beard shot back defiantly, "This is public land, Ranger. We got every right to be here."

Rachel's jaw tightened at the challenge, but she kept her voice steady. "I understand that, sir, but this is an active investigation. Your presence could compromise the evidence."

"Compromise?" scoffed a younger woman holding a toddler on her hip. "This ain't no courtroom drama, lady. We're just curious, is all."

As murmurs of agreement rippled through the crowd, Rachel knew it was pointless to argue with them any further. Work was over for the day, and a crime scene was as good as any TV show. And the crime scene was close enough to the town that it was attracting more passersby as the minutes ticked.

Rachel could feel frustration mounting, but refused to allow it purchase in her soul.

She'd have to work around their stubbornness or cause a scene. And the thought of causing a scene was distasteful to her.

"Fine," she conceded, mentally marking each face in the crowd before turning her attention to the task at hand. "Just stay behind the tape and don't touch anything."

With a deep breath, Rachel knelt down to examine the ground near the edge of the field. She ran her fingers gently over the dry dirt, feeling for any disturbances or markings that might indicate the victim's path. She catalogued details in her mind, constructing possible scenarios.

As she moved across the uneven terrain, she spotted a series of faint footprints leading away from the main cluster of onlookers. The prints were shallow and spaced closely together, suggesting someone had walked slowly, perhaps hesitantly, toward the center of the field.

Rachel mused, tracing the footsteps with her eyes. A sudden gust of wind stirred the tall grass, revealing a thin piece of fabric caught on a nearby thistle.

"Gotcha," she whispered, carefully dislodging the fabric with her gloved hand. She held it up to the fading sunlight, taking note of its color and texture.

A woman's dress. The victim?

Her eyes moved toward the body, which she hadn't approached yet. Police lined the space around the corpse, all of them muttering in quiet voices.

A strange atmosphere hung over the place.

Another death, as if the hands of a reaper had reached from a grave.

She stood up, slipping the fabric into an evidence bag. As she approached the body, she saw that it was a woman, her once-beautiful face now contorted in agony. Rachel felt a pang of sadness for the woman, who was no doubt someone's daughter, sister, or mother.

She knelt down beside the body, careful not to disrupt any of the evidence. She donned a fresh pair of gloves and began her preliminary examination. The woman's neck bore deep bruises, and her clothing was torn and bloodied. Rachel took note of these details as she worked.

The reason she'd been called was evident.

Black oil along the woman's lips, dribbling from each nostril, staining her clothing.

Drowned in oil.

Rachel shivered, staring at the apparent marks.

She studied the body more closely and then turned to look at the ground. The earth could tell tales that humans refused to allow past their lips.

She stared at the earth.

More footprints. Matching the ones she'd followed to the fabric.

She turned now, studying this trail, picking it out. To most, the footprints would've appeared like nothing more than mud. The faintest of lines here, the occasional tread mark there.

But to her trained eye, it told a story.

"Ranger Blackwood?" a police officer was saying behind her.

But she barely heard. She stood up and moved away from the body, her eyes attentive to every little indentation in the mud.

As she surveyed the scene, the first drops of rain began to fall. Rachel looked up; the moon had disappeared, swallowed by the heavy clouds. She could feel the moisture in the air, indicating that the rain would soon intensify. The storm had come quick, and now it seemed ready to unleash its fury upon the small town.

Better work fast before this rain washes away any more evidence, she thought, watching as two cops began pulling a plastic tarp from their trunk to cover the body. As the rain began to pelt down harder, she glanced back at the crowd of onlookers. Grudgingly, they were beginning to disperse, though a few of the more stubborn gawkers raised papers over their heads to block out the rain.

"Hey!" Rachel called out to one of the officers standing nearby. "I need you to preserve these tracks before the rain erases them!"

"Right away, Ranger Blackwood!" he replied, hurrying off to grab another tarp.

"Thanks," she said.

Rachel's eyes scanned the muddy ground surrounding the victim, her intuition urging her to dig deeper. She crouched down and ran her fingers through the soil, feeling its dampness and observing the way it clung to her fingertips.

She noticed something jutting out from under the woman. Rachel reached down and tugged a small billfold.

She slipped a plastic identification card from inside the wallet.

Her deep brown eyes scanned the information presented before her. The victim was Emily Thompson, thirty-two years old, working as a local schoolteacher. A gold band adorned her left ring finger—married, but no mention of children.

"Emily Thompson," Rachel repeated under her breath, committing the name to memory. As she slipped the ID back into its sheath, she couldn't help but feel a pang of sadness in her chest. This woman had a life, dreams, and people who cared for her. And now it was up to Rachel to bring justice to her memory.

"Forensic team's here, Ranger Blackwood," an officer informed her, snapping her out of her momentary reverie.

"Good. Let's get to work," Rachel replied, her determination burning like a wildfire as she directed the team to collect soil samples.

The raindrops continued to fall, and she could feel the water soaking through her clothing now.

But she ignored it.

The rain had always been a friend as far as she was concerned. The steady drops continued to fall, tapping on the brim of Rachel's Stetson like a funeral march. The drops slid down to the corners of her eyes, blurring the crime scene before her. Yet even through the veil of water, she could feel the weight of Emily Thompson's lifeless body.

"Ranger Blackwood," a voice called out, pulling her attention away from the grisly sight. An officer hurried toward her, his boots sinking into the damp earth with each step. "We've secured the area, and the citizens have been moved back."

"Good," Rachel replied, her eyes scanning the perimeter where the few townsfolk remaining had finally relented and retreated.

"Ma'am, do you need anyth—" the officer began, but his words were suddenly drowned out by the deafening crack of gunfire.

Rachel's heart leapt into her throat as she instinctively counted the shots—one… two… three—all in rapid succession. The sound echoed off the trees, making it difficult to discern the direction they came from.

But countless days spent tracking through the wilderness told her the shots had originated from somewhere to her right.

"Get down!" she shouted, her voice barely audible above the storm. She pushed the officer to the ground, diving behind the nearest patrol car for cover. Her pulse raced as adrenaline coursed through her veins, sharpening her senses.

Other officers were moving quickly now, reaching for their own weapons, scanning the tree line she'd indicated.

A pause. A shout.

And then another gunshot.

CHAPTER TWENTY FOUR

The sounds of the gunshots resounded in the still, desolate road outside the oil town.

The pitch-black sky hung heavily above them, pierced only by the glaring red and blue lights of the police cars. Rachel Blackwood's steely brown eyes scanned the scene before her from where she crouched low by a police cruiser.

The desert road outside the small oil town seemed to stretch endlessly into the darkness.

"Stand down!" a law enforcement officer shouted, his voice trembling with fear.

Her eyes were fixed on the figures in the tree line. In the dim light, Rachel saw a man gripping a gun, his face a mask of grief and desperation.

It took her a second to place the moving figures.

Two cops, both of them trying to calm the man.

The man looked like an oil worker. His gun was aimed at the sky, and a thin trail of smoke wafted past them, like a glaze of mist.

He was weeping, his hand trembling where he clutched his weapon.

Rachel stared, slowly emerging from where she crouched, frowning at the odd scene. The man kept his gun pointed at the sky.

He didn't strike her as an immediate threat.

But he was sobbing, and tears streaked down his face. He had soft features and long eyelashes that belied his upraised weapon and aggressive shouting.

She could just make out what he was saying.

His screams tore through the night, each word laced with anguish.

"Where is she?" he was yelling. "Where's Emily!"

Rachel stood up straight now, feeling a pit form in her stomach.

"Shit," she muttered under her breath. "It's the husband."

Ethan, who had crouched next to her, spit into the earth, further darkening a patch of soil wet from the rain.

Both of them knew this part of the job, and neither of them liked it.

The man was clearly beyond himself. He kept his gun raised above his head, but his finger was tightening, as if preparing to fire off another salvo at the rain clouds above.

The water continued to drum around them, tapping against the windshield of the car.

"Stay back," Rachel whispered to her partner, adjusting her leather jacket and bracing herself for action. She could feel the weight of her boots on the cracked ground, her muscles tensing like a coiled spring.

This man needed help, not more violence, she reasoned.

"Sir! Please put the gun down!" Rachel called out, her voice steady despite the chaos swirling around her. The man turned to her, startled, but didn't lower his weapon. She inched closer, holding up her hands in a gesture of peace.

"Who are you?" the man asked, tears streaming down his face.

"Rachel Blackwood, Texas Ranger," she replied, her words imbued with a quiet strength. "Now, please. Lower the gun."

The two cops had shuffled back briefly, shooting uncertain glances at her, both of them still holding their guns tightly.

She raised a hand at them as if she were attempting to quiet wild stallions.

The cops hesitantly lowered their guns, following her lead, but they kept their attention on the man. If he lowered his gun and aimed at them, it wouldn't end well.

She needed to prevent this from happening.

"Sir, I can talk to you about Emily," Rachel said quietly. "Mr. Thompson, what's your name?"

He stared at her, wide-eyed, pupils dilated. Fear emanated from his every motion.

"I…" He swallowed. "Callen."

"Alright, Callen, just lower the gun. Slowly, okay? We can talk about Emily. You'd like that, wouldn't you?"

She kept her tone even, gentle, as if she were speaking to a wounded creature.

As if sensing her sincerity, the man hesitated for a moment before slowly lowering the gun. The cops tensed as it reached shoulder height, but relaxed as it aimed at the ground. Rachel moved swiftly, closing the distance between them in an instant. With practiced precision, she disarmed him, securing the weapon.

The man didn't have time to react.

She didn't twist hard, though, not wanting to hurt him.

She didn't even focus on the weapon, as she didn't want Callen to either.

"Look at me, sir," she said quietly, meeting his gaze.

He did, his tear-stained eyes finding her calm, quiet countenance.

The other officers held back, watching as she reached out, touching his elbow lightly.

"Come with me, please."

He hesitated, but under the rain as it drummed around them, he slowly allowed her to guide him away.

Directly away from the body.

If he saw his wife in that state, there was no telling what he might do.

She led Callen Thompson gently away from the chaos, her firm grip on his arm offering both reassurance and restraint.

"Tell me about your wife," Rachel urged, her voice softening as they moved to a quieter spot beside one of the police cars. The man's breath hitched, his eyes welling up with fresh tears.

"Her name's Emily," he said, his voice barely audible. "She's everything to me. I heard… I heard she was here. Where is she?"

He looked around, peering in the back of the cop cars.

Shit. He didn't know she was dead.

"Focus on Emily for me," Rachel said, maintaining steady eye contact with the man. "What was she wearing when you last saw her?" She leaned in closer, her body language open and attentive.

"Uh, she had on a blue sundress, with little white flowers. And her favorite straw hat," he replied, his voice starting to steady as he recalled the details. "She always wore that hat when we went out."

"Good, that's good," Rachel encouraged, nodding along. "Now, did she have any communication with anyone suspicious? Any strange phone calls or messages?"

The man furrowed his brow, trying to remember. "Why… why are you asking me this? Is she here or not?"

His voice was growing more agitated.

Rachel redirected. "Anyone contact your wife? Anyone you can think of?"

"I… no. Just…" He trailed off, frowning.

She pointed sharply at him. "What did you just remember?"

"Just a phone call. Someone wanting to speak with her. I answered and he was… odd."

"Odd how?"

"Just off."

"Did you let him speak to your wife?"

"Hell no. He got angry."

"When was this?"

Callen was looking around the area, swallowing as he did. But at her words, he just shrugged. "I… I don't remember. Last week? Two weeks ago?"

"Can you recall anything specific about his voice?" Rachel asked, her mind already working through potential leads.

"Deep… and kind of raspy. He had an accent, too," the man said, struggling to pinpoint exactly what type of accent it was. "Maybe Southern? But not like Texas, more like… Louisiana, or Mississippi."

"Interesting," Rachel mused, filing away the information. She knew that accents could be faked, but it was still another piece of the puzzle. "Do you happen to remember the number he called from?"

"Blocked," he responded. "Now where the hell is my wife?"

Rachel reached out, gripping his shoulder tightly. She looked him in the eyes, and didn't say a word.

He met her gaze, staring.

Then he swallowed.

"No…" he whispered. He shook his head. "No… no, no…"

"I'm sorry. We found her a few hours ago."

"Where is she! Where's Emily?"

"She's gone, sir. Killed. You don't want to see her like this."

His legs gave out at her words and he collapsed like a marionette with snipped strings.

She tried to catch his arm to ease his fall, but there wasn't much she could do.

Rachel watched as Callen crumpled to the ground, his grief palpable. She stood silently, giving him the space he needed to process the news. The rain continued to fall around them, a steady drumbeat.

He didn't look up, didn't move. He lay there, weeping in the mud.

She felt the rain pouring down her face, and she reached out, patting him on the shoulder. She then nodded at the two cops who'd first spotted Callen. She gestured at them to approach.

She turned, and as they drew near, she murmured, "Get him someplace warm. Get him some food."

"Is he under arrest?"

"No. No, don't arrest him."

The cops nodded and moved over to help console Mr. Thompson.

Rachel turned away from the scene, shaking her head bitterly. She drew closer to Ethan.

"Find anything?" the tall southerner asked.

She stood by the side of the police cruiser, ducking under the umbrella Ethan had procured. She nodded as she did. "Yeah, I think so," she murmured, glancing back at Mr. Thompson. "Someone called his wife. Someone aggressive."

"Think they're the killer?"

"Very possibly," Rachel said softly. "We need to run his phone records. Find out who called. Where from."

Ethan gave a slow sad shake of his head, but turned back toward the car.

Rachel glanced once more at the body under the tarp, on the other side of the stationary vehicle. Then she turned back and slipped into the car, already pulling her phone to request the necessary information.

CHAPTER TWENTY FIVE

The Servant stood in the shadows of his small motel room, rain streaking down the windowpane like dark rivulets of blood. He raised his binoculars to his eyes, peering out at the crime scene illuminated by harsh police lights. Through the distorted lens, he saw Ranger Blackwood and Ranger Morgan climb into a cop car, their faces etched with determination and sorrow. He knew their faces now—knew their names. He'd been doing some digging of his own.

As the vehicle pulled away, the Servant's gaze lingered on a man standing near the perimeter of the crime scene. The man's face was contorted in anguish, hot tears streaming down his cheeks as he clung to the cold comfort of a nearby officer. The Servant felt a pang of empathy deep within him, an ache that gnawed at his conscience. It was an odd sensation for someone who considered himself a mere instrument of fate; it was a connection he had not anticipated feeling. He blinked away his own tears, swallowing the lump in his throat.

"Forgive me," he whispered, his voice barely audible over the pounding rain. "But I'm going to bleed again."

The scents and sounds of the night pierced through the atmosphere of the motel room: the musty odor of damp carpet, the distant wail of sirens, the relentless drumming of raindrops against the window. The man closed his eyes and breathed it all in, allowing the sensory feast to heighten his awareness and sharpen his focus.

His mind raced with thoughts of his next move, each detail meticulously planned and executed in his imagination. The familiar thrill coursed through his veins as he envisioned the terror and chaos that would soon unfold. Yet, mingled with this sinister excitement was a flicker of remorse, an unsettling reminder of the lives he had shattered.

"Bleed again? Yes, but only when the time is right," he told himself sternly, shaking off the lingering guilt. But even as he spoke these words, he knew that the urge to act was growing stronger, fueled by the conflict within him. The man's destiny was intertwined with those who crossed his path, and like a moth drawn to the flame, he could not resist the call of fate.

"Rachel," he murmured, the name rolling off his tongue like a dark incantation. "Ethan."

Their faces swam before his eyes, etched into his memory by the brief glimpse through the binoculars. He wondered what secrets lay hidden behind their stoic expressions, what unknown depths of pain and determination drove them forward. They were, in many ways, as much a mystery to him as he was to them.

But that would soon change. As the rain continued to fall outside the motel room window, the Servant prepared himself for the inevitable confrontation. And deep within the recesses of his heart, a small voice whispered a chilling truth: the day of reckoning was fast approaching.

He turned his attention to the small, flickering television set in the corner of the dingy motel room. The local news channel was broadcasting a report about his most recent crime. He leaned in closer, captivated by the grainy images of the scene he had left behind. The reporter's voice was hushed and somber, her words painting a vivid picture of the horror that had unfolded.

"Another gruesome discovery this evening as police uncovered the body of Emily Thompson, age thirty-two," she said, her face pale beneath the harsh glare of the camera lights. "Authorities have yet to release details, but sources close to the investigation suggest it bears striking similarities to the string of unsolved murders that have plagued the area in recent weeks."

The killer watched with interest as the camera panned across the crime scene, lingering on the flashing lights of the police cars and the grim expressions of the officers. A thrill coursed through him at the thought that he remained a specter to them—a phantom whose true nature eluded their grasp.

"Still no closer to catching me, are they?" he mused, a wicked smile playing upon his lips. His long, slender fingers tapped rhythmically against the arm of the rickety wooden chair, betraying his eagerness to continue his work. His clothing was nondescript, designed to blend into the shadows—a dark hoodie concealing his face, with worn jeans and scuffed boots completing the ensemble.

"Two more hours… yes, two hours should be enough time to prepare." His voice was barely more than a whisper, but it held an undeniable note of excitement. In his mind's eye, he saw the faces of Rachel and Ethan once more. They were connected to this twisted tapestry of fate he wove, and he knew that their paths would cross again soon.

He reached for his bag and pulled out a wickedly sharp knife. The blade gleamed in the dim light, reflecting the twisted desires that burned within his soul.

"Time to get to work," he murmured, his eyes glittering with cold determination. He cleaned and sharpened the knife with meticulous precision, each stroke bringing him closer to the moment when he would once again stand over his prey, consumed by the intoxicating power that washed over him in those final moments of life.

"Rachel, Ethan," he whispered, tasting their names on his tongue as he plunged the knife into the air, imagining the terror they would feel when they realized how close he had been all along. "Your time is coming."

As the television continued to drone on in the background, the Servant prepared himself for the deadly dance that lay ahead. And as he slipped silently from the motel room and into the night, the shadows embraced him, welcoming their dark emissary into their midst.

CHAPTER TWENTY SIX

The clock on the dingy interrogation room wall read 10:37 p.m., its ticking a steady rhythm in the otherwise silent precinct. Rachel sat hunched over a desk that had seen better days, her fingers tapping restlessly as she scanned the phone records of Mr. Thompson. The dim light overhead cast shadows across her face, deepening the lines of concentration that furrowed her brow.

"Dammit," she muttered under her breath.

"Anything yet?" Ethan asked quietly, his voice breaking through the silence. He leaned against the doorframe, concern etched into his features as he watched his partner tirelessly pursue the phone records.

"Maybe…" Rachel replied. "Most of the calls are local. A few are from spammers. But…" Her cursor hovered on the screen over a few calls from a week before. "These calls… they're different. Not from any known contacts. Not any listed business. Not known spam. Could be a connection."

"Can you trace them back to a location?" Ethan questioned, stepping closer to get a better look at the computer screen.

"I'm… not sure. It's not leading me…" She trailed off as Ethan nudged at her hand insistently.

She allowed him access to the keyboard.

"Lemme see if homicide has turned off my passcode yet."

He cycled to a separate database, and Rachel scooted back, watching, impressed, as the ex-homicide-detective-now-Ranger tapped away.

He opened a new portal on the webpage and clicked his tongue. "Which date was it again? Oh—yeah. Never mind. I see it."

Ethan's fingers flew over the keyboard, typing with practiced efficiency.

Suddenly, the local area code appeared on the screen, and Rachel felt a surge of excitement.

"Got it," Ethan said. "It's a local number." He stepped back, beaming as Rachel scrutinized the screen. She could tell he was proud of himself, but she also didn't want to burst his bubble.

"Nice," she said simply. She read the number twice, committing it to memory.

"Good work," Ethan praised, relief evident in his tone. "We should follow up on this first thing in the morning."

"No, we're doing this now." Rachel's gaze met Ethan's. "I can't let this monster take another victim."

"Rachel, it's late. We're both exhausted."

"Every minute counts," she countered, grabbing her hat and jacket as she stood up.

But she hesitated, glancing back at the screen. "What's this?"

"Huh?"

"This second link. Under the first."

He leaned in. "Oh. Huh. Shit."

"What?"

Ethan's gaze never left the screen. "This number connects to our suspect, but it was used from two different locations. A cellphone tower pinged both calls."

"Two?"

"Two primary locations, yeah. Two home addresses."

"Why two?"

He shrugged. Then looked at her. "Still wanna tackle this tonight?"

"Divide and conquer," she said resolutely. "I'll go to one address while you check out the other. We can cover more ground that way."

"I mean… you sure?"

Rachel nodded resolutely. It would be like old times. Tracking a predator through rough terrain, isolated and with only her wits for guidance.

She tried not to smile at the thought.

***

The first address led Rachel to a quaint suburban home, its exterior bathed in the warm glow of soft exterior lights. She parked her car a short distance away and cautiously approached the residence, her heart pounding in her ears. The scent of freshly cut grass hung heavy in the air, mingling with the subtle aroma of burning shrubs drifting from a neighbor's backyard as they attempted to bypass city ordinance by disposing of refuse under the cover of night and ash.

She approached the small house, moving slowly, a frown creasing her features.

The homes were both owned by the same landlord. A man named Deacon Miles. This, she supposed, might explain the phone records from the two homes.

But Deacon's number was unlisted, and she felt a faint tremor, wondering what awaited her within those walls.

She approached up the driveway, stray gravel crunching underfoot.

As she peered through the living room window, Rachel spotted only darkness. The lights in the house were off.

She paused, her mind flitting back to a happier time in her own family's life.

She tried not to dwell too much on all that had been lost.

But she found a knot forming in her stomach, and forced the thoughts aside with a faint harumph.

She knocked on the door, steeling herself for what might lie beyond it.

It was nearly midnight now.

No one responded to the knock.

She tried again, more insistently.

She rang the bell.

And could hear the faint bell ringing within. Another few seconds, and she heard movement within; muffled voices and shuffling footsteps.

Rachel drew her gun, her instincts telling her to be cautious. She pressed herself against the wall beside the door, waiting for whoever was inside to make their move.

After a few tense moments, the door creaked open, revealing a middle-aged man with a balding head and a thick beard. He seemed surprised to see her, and was blinking sleep from his eyes. "Can I help you?" he asked, his voice low and gravelly. He hadn't spotted the gun concealed by her hip yet.

"I'm with the Texas Rangers," Rachel said, her gaze flickering over the man's features. "Who are you?"

The man's eyes narrowed, suspicion etched into the lines of his face. "Got some ID?"

She was already in the middle of raising it before the question had completely left his lips.

He nodded once after scrutinizing the badge. "So what's up?" he said.

She stepped away from the door, her gun holstered now, but her hand still lingering on it. She looked the man up and down.

"Are you Deacon Miles?"

He scowled. "No. That's my landlord. He do something?"

"We're investigating a homicide case. Your address came up."

He stared at her, and even glanced past her, as if expecting to see someone standing there with a camera.

"This a joke?"

She just shook her head, her dark eyes boring into his, the thin trail of beads braided into her hair shifting under her hat.

"I don't know anything about that," he said, his tone defensive.

"Can I come inside?" Rachel asked, her gun still holstered.

He hesitated. "Can't this wait?"

"I'm afraid not."

"Shit. Can I see that badge again?"

She complied, polite but persistent.

Finally, he sighed, shrugged, then stepped back, allowing Rachel to enter the house. She moved cautiously through the dark interior, her senses on high alert.

The man led her to a small living room, where a woman perched on a well-worn couch, her eyes darting nervously at the newcomer. She was wearing a nightgown, and had a phone clutched in one hand and a baseball bat in the other.

"Who are you?" the woman demanded, her voice trembling.

"Hello, ma'am. I apologize for bothering you so late at night." Rachel brought out her professional tone and ID before it was requested this time. "I'm Texas Ranger Rachel Blackwood, and I have a few questions regarding your husband's whereabouts earlier this evening," she said, her voice steady and authoritative despite the uneasy feeling that gnawed at her gut.

The man's face paled slightly, but he quickly regained his composure. "My whereabouts?"

His wife was staring at him, confusion crawling across her features.

He stuttered at first, like a plane with a wobbly takeoff, but then calmed enough to stammer out, "I've been here all evening—my wife can confirm that," he insisted, glancing back at the woman, whose hands were twisting in her lap where she sat on the couch.

"Is this true?" Rachel said, watching the wife.

The woman nodded adamantly. "Yes. We've been watching *NCIS* reruns all night!"

Rachel frowned. "I need to ask you about a couple phone calls."

The man shrugged. “Sure. I’m an open book.” He frowned at her, but then turned and fetched a phone from the end table.

“Is this your only phone?”

“Yes!” the wife called out. “I would know if he had another.”

The man just nodded.

Rachel quickly checked the device’s number.

Not a match.

She cursed under her breath, but then forced a more relaxed expression. She turned back toward the two figures by the couch. She said, “I need an accounting for your movements over the last two weeks, sir.”

He stared at her. “I mean… work mostly. I haven’t missed.”

“And where do you work?”

“In the city. It’s an hour commute. Took today off to spend it with my wife.” He frowned at her.

Rachel was beginning to grow uneasy. The man didn’t look like someone hiding guilt. He looked like an irritated citizen trying to get back to sleep.

Rachel rocked on her heels. Suddenly, the man perked up. “I drive a tourist van,” he said. “And it’s equipped with GPS. Look, my phone tracks my whereabouts.”

He eagerly tapped an app on his phone and turned it so she could see.

Part of Rachel found she didn’t want to look. Dread was now crawling up inside her.

She knew before she looked it would check out. This man and his wife were tired and cranky.

But they weren’t guilt-ridden.

Shit.

She checked the app all the same, watching as he pulled up data logs of his GPS coordinates on site. She’d have to double-check with the company in the morning, but he was in the city, more than an hour away, when the bodies would’ve been dumped, and when the mechanic had been contacted by the killer to drop the corpses in the oil fields.

It wasn’t him.

Rachel took a screenshot of the data, then nodded at them both.

“Sorry for the inconvenience,” she said. “Do you recognize this number?”

She showed the number she’d found. But both of the figures on the couch shook their heads.

Suddenly, the silence was peeled back by a ringing sound.

She jolted, but realized her phone was buzzing. She hesitated only briefly before giving a curt nod to the couple and turning on her heel, hastening back toward the door.

Stepping back out into the driveway, she answered quickly, hoping for good news on her partner's end. "Ethan, what did you find?"

"Rachel, my guy is missing," he said, his voice tense and urgent. "Neighbors say they haven't seen him for days. I'm starting to think we might be too late."

"Damn it," Rachel cursed under her breath, her determination flaring anew. "Stay put, Ethan. I'm on my way," she said, already climbing into her car and starting the engine.

CHAPTER TWENTY SEVEN

The moon hung low, casting a ghostly silver glow over the desolate Texas highway as Rachel's black SUV devoured miles of asphalt. The rhythmic hum of tires on the road was interrupted only by the crackle of static from the police radio. Rachel's gaze darted between the rearview mirror and the dark expanse ahead.

"Any update, Ethan?" she asked, her voice steady and focused as she gripped the wheel with one hand and held the phone to her ear with the other.

"Dammit, Rachel," came the reply through the speakers, a mix of frustration and urgency. "APB got a hit, guy named Allen Boyd lives at the address I was going to, but when I showed up, Boyd saw me. He's taken off in his Corvette, headed east."

"Copy that. I'll intercept him," she said, her jaw set.

Rachel pressed down on the accelerator, urging her vehicle to close the distance.

"Stay on his tail, Ethan. Keep me posted on his speed and position," she commanded, her eyes narrowing with resolve.

"Got it," Ethan replied, the sound of his engine roaring in the background.

As the SUV's headlights cut through the darkness, illuminating the foreboding landscape, Rachel felt a surge of adrenaline coursing through her veins. Every muscle in her lithe runner's build tensed, ready for action.

The desolate Texas highway stretched out before her, an ebony ribbon slicing through the darkness, illuminated only by the fierce beams of her headlights.

"Rachel, he's taken a left onto Route 64," Ethan's voice crackled over the radio, his breath heavy with exertion. "He's really gunning it now."

"Alright, I'm coming up on the intersection at County Road 9," she replied, her knuckles white against the steering wheel. Every muscle in her body screamed for action, urging her to reach that crucial crossroads. Her mind raced, calculating distances and speeds in a frenetic dance of logistics. To catch Allen Boyd, she had to be precise, fearless, and above all else, fast. She could hear the undercurrent of urgency in her own voice, but there was no room for doubt or hesitation.

"Copy that," came Ethan's terse response, the sound of screeching tires faintly audible in the background. "Speed's around 110, heading east."

"Okay, I'm almost at the intersection. Get ready to box him in," Rachel said, her heart pounding like a tribal drum.

Her SUV roared into the empty crossroads, the tires gripping the asphalt with ferocious intensity as she slammed on the brakes, skidding to a halt just beyond the intersection.

"Rachel, he's approaching fast. Be ready!" Ethan warned, his words punctuated by the high-pitched whine of the suspect's sports car.

"I'm ready," she whispered, her eyes hard and unflinching.

The dark Texas night was shattered by the approaching blaring sirens and flashing red and blue lights, casting eerie shadows across the desolate landscape. Rachel's hands gripped the wheel of her black SUV, knuckles white with determination.

And then she spotted them.

The lights had been a siren's call, heralding the approach, but the bright red flash of metallic paint under street lights caught her eye.

The Corvette buzzed toward her, outpacing the police vehicles behind it.

Rachel tensed, stalled in the intersection, hands on the steering wheel as she waited for the vehicle to reach her.

She didn't flinch, as if she were staring down a charging bull.

"Come on," she whispered under her breath. "Come on!" Her hands tightened around the steering wheel, and she went strangely tense. For a moment, it almost felt as if the windshield were the glass on a sniper's scope. The red Corvette an animal caught in her crosshairs.

But sometimes, the hunter became the prey.

The red Corvette wasn't veering. It kept hurtling directly toward her.

She tensed. It would veer.

It had to veer.

It was a life-and-death game of chicken.

If she stayed put, and he slammed into her, she'd be turned into goo.

But if she moved, he'd speed right past her.

"Rachel!" Ethan's voice shouted through the speakers.

But she ignored him. She didn't move. It wasn't the thing to be done.

A phrase her aunt often uttered. The *thing to be done* was a sort of catch-all that explained a choice that seemed to have no explanation.

The red Corvette was fifty yards away. Twenty.

Coming so fast, she barely had time to blink.

But she didn't move.

He'd veer.

He would *have to* veer.

"Rachel!" Ethan shouted.

Her legs tensed, her jaw set.

And at the very last second, the red sports car turned sharply. The Corvette swerved to the right, tires screeching as it narrowly avoided Rachel's SUV. She watched as the red car attempted to careen past her, but the turn was too tight. He'd left it too late.

His vehicle's tires wailed against the asphalt as his front bumper slammed into a railing. Glass and sparks exploded, scattering across the ground.

Rachel let out a deep breath, her hands shaking slightly from the adrenaline rush. She had been so focused on the chase that she had forgotten to breathe.

Now, though, as she inhaled and shoved out of her car, her booted feet hitting the asphalt, she nearly choked on the breeze.

The acrid scent of burning rubber and gasoline filled the air from where the red sports car had come to a screeching halt, its mangled metal frame twisted and warped. Billowing plumes of smoke rose from the wreckage, accompanied by a symphony of shattered glass and debris that rained down like a violent hailstorm.

"Blackwood, are you okay?" Ethan's voice crackled through the radio, urgency punctuating every syllable.

"Fine," she replied as she began moving toward the waiting vehicle.

She approached cautiously, her weapon drawn.

She could feel the heat of the crash radiating against her skin, her boots crunching on gravel strewn across the asphalt.

Suddenly, there was another screeching sound, and an unmarked car skidded across the asphalt.

In an impressive display of coordination, Ethan launched from the front seat just as it came to a stop, the sound of his rapid footfalls replacing the screech of rubber on gravel.

He hurried toward her, giving her a quick once-over.

She flashed a thumbs-up. "Fine," she repeated.

He nodded, looking relieved.

The two of them had their weapons raised now, both of them shoulder to shoulder, moving in tandem as they closed in on the crippled car, their guns aimed at the shattered windows and the still form of Allen Boyd slumped inside. Rachel could see blood staining his face, a stark contrast to the pale complexion beneath. The flames arose around the car, coming from the front. Soon, the fire would reach the driver, and then there would be no interrogation.

Without hesitation, Rachel rushed toward the car. She could feel the heat of the flames on her skin as she reached the driver's side door. The metal was twisted and warped, making it impossible to open. She banged on the window, but it wouldn't budge. Smoke filled her lungs, making it difficult to breathe. She could hear Ethan shouting, but his words were muffled by the roar of the flames. She had to act fast. There was no time to waste.

Taking a step back, Rachel raised her gun and aimed at the window, away from Boyd's face. Three shots rang out, shattering the glass. She reached in and unlocked the door, pulling it open with all her might. Flames licked at her sleeve where they wafted over the windshield. Inside the car was still safe—but not for much longer. She was focused on getting Allen Boyd out of the car.

Suddenly, she tensed.

Hunters were trained to note even the smallest of motions.

And she caught it, just then. A flutter of eyelashes. A faint inhale.

She began to pull back, shouting a warning.

But in a sudden burst of movement, Allen Boyd's hand shot toward the glove compartment. Rachel's heart hammered in her chest as she barked out a warning: "Don't do it, Boyd!"

Ethan reacted instantly, lunging through the opposite window where he'd circled around. His hand smashed through the glass, and he grabbed Boyd's wrist just as it made contact with the cold steel of a hidden gun. The two men grappled for control, their bodies twisting and limbs flailing in the cramped space.

"Drop it!" Ethan gasped, sweat beading his brow as he strained against the suspect's surprising strength.

Rachel didn't hesitate, her boots scuffing on the gravel as she aimed a sharp punch at Boyd's shoulder. The impact sent pain shooting up her arm, but it did the trick—the man crumpled, releasing his grip on the weapon as he cried out in pain.

Rachel quickly grabbed the gun, making sure to keep it pointed away from both Ethan and Boyd. She could feel the heat of the flames getting closer and knew they needed to get out of there.

"Let's go!" she shouted, grabbing Boyd by the back of his shirt and pulling him out of the car. Ethan followed close behind, his hand on the small of Rachel's back as they hurried away from the burning wreckage.

They made it just in time as the flames hit the fuel and the car detonated, sending a wave of heat and debris flying toward them. Rachel shielded her face with her arm, feeling the force of the explosion rock her to her core. There must've been something extra, she realized. Nitro? Some sort of street racing additive?

As the flames began to die down, she turned to Boyd who was gasping at the ground, shaking his head in frustration and muttering a series of insults.

"Amy!" he yelled.

She realized he was grieving his car.

Ethan moved around behind the kneeling man, cuffs in hand. "Don't move!" Ethan snapped.

The wail of sirens continued to approach, drawing nearer.

Rachel took a deep breath, her heart still pounding from the adrenaline rush. They had caught Boyd, but the chase had left her feeling raw and exposed. She could feel the sweat on her skin and the grit in her teeth as she surveyed the scene. The wreckage of the car lay twisted and smoking, a testament to the danger they faced.

Rachel knew that they had been lucky this time. If the car had hit her head-on, she might not have made it out alive.

But he'd veered.

She'd made the call, and she'd been right. This time.

Ethan was speaking into his radio, his voice low and urgent. Rachel could hear the distant sound of approaching sirens, the cavalry on its way. She looked around, taking in the scene—the burnt-out car, the twisted metal, the shattered glass—and felt a twinge of sadness.

She pictured the victims. Soaked in oil, just like the Corvette was now.

As the sound of the sirens grew louder, Rachel turned to Ethan. "Let's get him out of here before we have to tangle with local PD for jurisdiction."

Ethan nodded, his eyes scanning the wreckage one last time before he helped pull Boyd to his feet.

The cuffed man did little to protest, still scowling as he was pushed forward, ushered toward Ethan's waiting vehicle.

CHAPTER TWENTY EIGHT

The dimly lit interrogation room seemed to close in on itself, creating an oppressive atmosphere that weighed heavily upon its occupants. A single flickering fluorescent bulb cast a pallid glow over the sparse furnishings: a cold metal table and two chairs that looked like they'd been through one too many interrogations themselves. Rachel sat across from Boyd, who was handcuffed to the table.

Boyd was every inch the street racer—lean, muscular, with angular features that gave him a predatory air. His dark hair was slicked back, revealing a tattoo of a black panther that snaked up his neck and behind his ear. His eyes were a piercing green, framed by a pair of dark, arched eyebrows that lent him an aura of defiance. Beneath the surface, however, there was an undercurrent of fear that couldn't quite be hidden. Sweat glistened on his brow, and his hands trembled ever so slightly as they gripped the edge of the table. A faint cut stretched across his forehead, down to the corner of his jaw.

"Look, I ain't sayin' another word till my lawyer's here," Boyd rasped, his voice hoarse and shaky. The tension in the room grew palpable.

"Fine," Rachel replied, her voice steady and calm despite the growing pressure.

Boyd glanced at her for a moment, then quickly averted his gaze, swallowing hard. "I want… I want my lawyer," he repeated, his voice barely above a whisper now.

Rachel leaned back in her chair and narrowed her eyes, studying Boyd's nervous demeanor. His forehead was sheened with sweat, and he darted his eyes around the dimly lit room like a cornered animal searching for an escape.

"I'm not going to ask you any questions," she said slowly. She reached up, plucking her hat off her head and lowering it onto the table next to her.

His eyes followed it.

"I just think better speaking out loud," she said.

She turned away from him, as if she were addressing the mirror. "And I wonder," she said slowly, "if it's true that a phone call was made from your address to one of our murder victims. In fact, multiple phone calls."

He tensed. "Hang on…"

"Hush," she said, frowning at him. "I'm not talking to you. You want your lawyer, remember?"

She looked away from him again. Then, in a softer voice, as if she were simply musing aloud, she said, "I wonder why it is that Boyd might have made those calls… and with his criminal record? It's certainly a checkered past."

"Now wait just a minute!" snapped the street racer.

She continued. "And he *still* flouts the law. Nearly creating a collision with the police. He'd rather flee than face what he's done. Yes." She nodded gravely. "Yes, yes—I can't help but think he must be involved somehow."

At the sound of her voice, Boyd flinched, as if her words physically hurt him. His hands shook violently, rattling the handcuffs against the metal table. Rachel couldn't help but wonder what had caused such a visceral reaction in him.

"Please," Boyd whispered, his voice cracking under the strain. "I can't… I don't know anything."

"Then why are you so scared?" Rachel asked, her tone gentle yet probing. She leaned forward slightly, trying to catch his gaze. "We all make mistakes, Boyd. It's how we learn and grow. But we can't move past them unless we face them head-on."

For a fleeting moment, his eyes locked onto hers, and Rachel saw a glimmer of something—desperation, perhaps, or even hope—before he quickly looked away again. The fear was still stamped across his face, but there was the slightest hint of determination now as well.

"Look, I… I just need my lawyer, okay?" Boyd said, his voice steadier than before, though still tinged with anxiety. "Then maybe… maybe we can sort this out."

Rachel sighed inwardly as she tried to decipher the enigma that was Boyd.

The silence in the room was thick, as though the air itself had become heavy with anxiety. Rachel's gaze remained fixed on Boyd. She didn't say a word, but just *watched* him, her penetrating gaze piercing him to his chair.

Boyd shifted uneasily, his handcuffed hands gripping the metal table before him. He avoided eye contact with Rachel, instead directing his gaze at a crack in the cold concrete floor beneath them. "I've told you already, I don't know anything," he muttered weakly, his voice barely audible.

A glimpse of the truth hidden behind those fearful eyes.

As if on cue, the door to the interrogation room swung open, revealing a tall, imposing woman with a no-nonsense attitude. She entered the room with purpose, her heels clicking against the floor as she approached the table. Boyd visibly relaxed upon seeing her, his fidgeting coming to an abrupt halt.

"Victoria Caldwell," the woman introduced herself, though no one had asked. She set her briefcase down on the table with a decisive *click*. "I'm Mr. Boyd's attorney." She shot Boyd a reassuring glance before turning her attention back to Rachel. "I understand you've been questioning my client without legal representation present?"

Rachel bristled at the accusation, but bit back any retort that threatened to spill from her lips. Instead, she opted to remain silent, her jaw clenched tightly as she watched Victoria take a seat beside Boyd.

Her eyes briefly moved to a second figure standing in the hall. A man. He was dressed in a neat suit, and had begun pulling a pack of cigarettes from his pocket.

"My chauffeur," the lawyer said quickly. "Don't mind him."

The door was swinging slowly shut on spring-loaded hinges. To Rachel's eye, the man out in the hall looked more like a bodyguard than a chauffeur. She wondered what sort of law firm she was dealing with.

One that paid its employees well, no doubt. The man in the hall was wearing an expensive suit, and his shoes caught her attention. Also expensive, with a unique, golden swoop on the sides.

The sort of outfit one might give someone to keep quiet. The mob often plied its members with gifts to keep them in line.

The door shut now, sealing off Rachel's view, and she returned her attention to the present threat.

"Alright then," Victoria said, her voice calm yet firm. "Let's get started, shall we?"

Rachel's eyes narrowed as the lawyer, Victoria, surveyed the room with an air of authority. The silence in the dimly lit space was broken by the sound of her briefcase clicking open and a stack of papers being rustled.

"Ranger," Victoria said, her voice cold and unyielding, "I must ask you to leave the room. Your presence could be considered coercion."

The lawyer spoke smoothly, not even bothering to look up from her papers. "I'll handle everything from here."

Rachel shrugged, giving Boyd a long look. She got to her feet and pushed out the door. The hallway was dimly lit, casting long shadows that only served to heighten her sense of unease. She paced back and forth, her mind racing, before finally stopping in front of the one-way mirror that offered a view into the room.

From this vantage point, she watched Boyd's trembling hands and darting eyes as he spoke in hushed tones with Victoria.

Why had he fled? Because he'd known they'd caught up with him?

Was this timid, scared street racer really the killer?

It made sense. Behind a steering wheel, or the blade of a knife, perhaps he felt powerful. But faced with danger?

Not so much.

The dim light from the overhead bulb cast solemn shadows across Boyd's face, emphasizing the dark circles under his weary eyes. He leaned in closer to Victoria, his chained wrists clanking softly against the metal table. Their conversation was hushed, each word exchanged like a precious secret, too fragile for the open air.

She studied Boyd, the nervous way he kept drumming his fingers against the table. His shifting posture, his gaze darting furtively toward the closed door.

This was a man who was hiding something.

But what?

She crossed her arms, watching.

Was he the killer?

Cops were back at his place, combing through everything. But no call meant nothing found…

Yet.

Still… she frowned, feeling a cold shiver.

The lawyer was still talking to her client, but that didn't mean Rachel had to stand idly by.

Besides, they had the man's phone.

The phone that had supposedly made the call.

She frowned in the direction of the tattooed fellow. Her eyes traced the neck tattoo, moving down to his sleeve.

She hesitated.

A date.

Important enough to etch indelibly on his skin…

She stared at the numbers. 12.12.

Did it mean anything?

More importantly…

Her eyes widened.

She felt a flicker of excitement.

Would it unlock his phone?

Important enough to tattoo meant important enough to remember. Boyd didn't exactly seem like a brainiac.

She turned away from the mirror, moving swiftly now toward the evidence room, a hitch in her step.

CHAPTER TWENTY NINE

The man drummed his fingers against the steering wheel, watching as rain came down in sheets.

In one hand, he held a knife.

His pants were in the back seat.

He stared down at his thighs, frowning at the scars tracing the inside of his leg.

He tapped the knife against the old scars, slowly tracing the outline with the tip of the blade.

It caused shivers to creep along his back, a sort of giddy anticipation.

He traced the scars with practiced precision, knowing them intimately. His knife moved up and down in an undulating motion.

The drumming of the rain against his windshield gave him a brief surge of excitement.

He licked his lips.

Through the glass, through the doors, he spotted the police station.

They were all in there.

Squawking like a bunch of chickens. Squawking about him, no doubt.

He'd wanted to wait for this next target. Had wanted to give it time… It had taken so very long to set it all up, anyway.

But now… No. Now he was determined. He'd made up his mind.

He continued to trace his thighs with the knife, remembering the wounds and how they'd been inflicted.

His scars reminded him of tree roots, dug deep into the soil, soaking up essential minerals and nutrients.

The ground was a stabilizing force to him.

He let out a faint shuddering sigh.

And then someone tapped on his window.

He stiffened, pretending he hadn't heard at first.

A hand tapped a bit more insistently.

He turned slowly.

A police officer was staring in through his window, frowning at the man.

The man didn't flinch. He simply looked up at the officer with a blank expression, the knife still in his hand.

"Sir, is there a problem? You can't just park here," the officer said, his hand resting on the holster of his gun.

The man's eyes flickered to the gun, then back to the officer's face. He gave a small smile, but it was a smile that didn't reach his eyes.

"No problem, Officer. Just waiting for someone," he said, his voice smooth and calm.

The officer narrowed his eyes, looking at the man with suspicion. "Mind if I take a look inside your car?" he asked. His eyes glanced toward the discarded pants. How embarrassing.

The man's grip on the knife tightened. He knew he couldn't let the officer search the car.

"I'm sorry, Officer, but I can't let you do that," he said, his voice even colder than before.

The cop paused, as if taken aback. "You sure about that, buddy?" he said, frowning.

The cop was a young man, with handsome, pale features. His face was clean-shaven, and his uniform was crisp and clean. The man in the car felt a twinge of jealousy at the sight of the officer's youth and vitality.

"I'm sure," the man said, his voice low. "I'm a private person, you know?"

"I can't help but notice…" The cop's eyes moved to the knife, then to the scars on the driver's legs. "What's going on here?"

"Just a little ritual," said the man in the car. He didn't try to hide it. What would be the point of that? Instead, he said it firmly, with a finality in his tone, daring the cop to question him further.

"I see… And what sort of ritual is that?"

The man in the car smiled again, the same smile that didn't reach his eyes. "It's a personal one. You wouldn't understand," he said, his voice dropping to a whisper.

The cop's hand tightened on his gun. "I'm going to have to ask you to step out of the car."

The man in the car hesitated for a moment, his eyes flickering to the police station once again. But he knew he couldn't risk it. Not now. Not when he was so close to fulfilling his plan.

He opened the car door slowly, the knife still in his hand, and stepped out into the pouring rain. The cop moved to search him, but the man shook his head. "I don't have anything on me," he said, holding his hands up in surrender.

"Please drop the knife," the cop said.

The man from the car nodded slowly, but glanced in the direction of the precinct.

No one was watching.

No one could see.

Not until they checked the security footage, and by then it would all be over.

So he released his grip on the knife.

It fell, and the moment it struck the ground, he lunged at the cop, moving fast.

He slammed into the smaller man, bringing him crashing to the ground.

The breath whooshed from both of them as they hit the concrete hard. The cop's gun went skittering across the ground, under another car.

The cop tried to gouge at the man's eyes, but it was too late.

Far, far too late for any of that.

He was heavier, larger. He wrapped his fingers around the cop's neck and began squeezing.

There was something exhilarating about strangling a police officer just outside the precinct.

No one called out. No one shouted.

The wind and the rain and the cover of clouds served to disguise the events on the asphalt.

The cop gurgled, grabbing at the man's hands, trying to snap a finger.

But it was no use.

The man was relentless, pushing his thumbs deeper into the cop's throat.

The cop kicked up, catching the man between the legs. He let out a pained yelp and nearly fell off. The cop was going for his Taser now.

But the man redoubled his efforts, ignoring the lancing pain shooting through his gut.

He grabbed at the cop a second time as the officer surged to his feet. But he pulled the cop back to the ground, dragging him to the soaking cement.

The cop squirmed and kicked, but he was no match for the man's strength.

The man squeezed his fingers around the officer's throat. He watched the light in the cop's eyes, staring at the youthful, handsome features.

There was something almost poetic about the moment. Something that sent shivers up his spine.

"It'll be over now," he whispered, his voice panting.

The man's grip tightened, and the cop's body went limp beneath him. The man held on for a while longer, savoring the feeling of power that coursed through his veins. He was a god, he realized. He held the power of life and death in his hands. And it was intoxicating.

Slowly, he released his grip on the cop's throat and crawled backwards, panting heavily. He watched the rain wash over the cop's body. It was a beautiful sight.

But the cop was still breathing.

He stared at the faint rising and falling of the unconscious man's chest.

He was young. Fresh.

The earth didn't need him. Not now.

He would allow the man to live.

Yes… yes, he'd decided. But he needed to hide the man's body.

The man stood up shakily, feeling invigorated by the fight. He picked up the knife from the ground and wiped it on his pants so it wouldn't rust.

The man looked around, breathing heavily. No one had seen anything. He tucked the knife back into his pocket.

He then bent over and grabbed at the unconscious cop's form. He had some spare rope in the trunk, and there was an alley across the street with some large dumpsters. He'd have to be quick, of course.

But the fact that this was all outside a police station, and they hadn't seen a damn thing in the storm, only further excited him.

He moved quickly, grabbing the cop, pushing him into the front seat, and then hastening around the back to grab rope from the trunk.

All the while, he couldn't help but feel a rising sense of certainty.

They would emerge from the precinct soon.

They would not expect a thing.

And when they came, he'd be waiting.

It was time.

He'd waited long enough, but it was time for it all to be over.

CHAPTER THIRTY

Once inside the evidence room, Rachel approached the desk where the confiscated items were kept, moving hurriedly, her eyes like a hawk's fixated on her target, neither swiveling to the left nor the right.

She reached the desk and snatched the green, plastic folder with large pockets, dividing the different partitions. She flipped through the folder containing Boyd's belongings until she found the phone. It was a cheap, old model, but it was still functional. She pressed the power button, and the screen lit up. It prompted her for a passcode.

She hesitated, glanced over her shoulder at the empty hall, then shrugged. Nothing ventured, nothing gained. Sometimes it was best not to overthink it, but just to take the damn shot.

She typed 1212.

And waited.

The screen unlocked, and she smirked, feeling a sudden thrill of satisfaction.

She began cycling through the old phone, going into the call logs and searching for past calls. Her eyes took in every detail, not wanting to miss a single thing.

She cycled back to the date when the calls had been placed to their most recent victim.

She paused.

There it was.

He hadn't even cleared his recent calls.

Three outgoing calls placed. All of them to the same number. Emily Thompson's number.

"Holy shit," she said, her hand gripping the device and a grin stretching across her features.

She frowned, though, pausing as she stood there.

What sort of mastermind criminal called someone on their own phone?

Why had similar calls been placed from a *second* address? She pulled out her own phone.

She entered Boyd's information and then paused.

"Well… there we go."

Occupation. Maintenance.

He worked as a maintenance worker for his landlord's properties. That's why he would've been at *both* addresses; he apparently also just happened to live at one of them.

"So why aren't you satisfied?" she murmured.

No one else was in the room to hear the question. And yet it gnawed at her.

Why indeed.

She bit her lower lip, staring at the phone. The killer had hired someone to hide the bodies. Had existed like a wraith in darkness, hidden from sight.

So why would he have come out into the open *now*?

She hesitated, staring at the phone.

She bit her lip.

And then she cycled back in the call logs. *Before* the calls were placed to Emily Thompson.

She stared at the information logged there, her eyes narrowed briefly.

Another number. This one an unknown caller.

Someone had called Boyd before he'd placed the calls to Emily's number.

And now, like a hound with a scent, Rachel shifted her focus. Instead of lingering on the phone, she cycled to one of the cash apps.

Her finger hovered over it, and she paused. Part of her didn't even *want* to know.

But she sighed, exhaling deeply. She clicked the app.

It didn't take long to find the transaction.

A lump sum of a thousand dollars deposited into Boyd's account right before he placed the calls to Mrs. Thompson.

"Shit," she muttered under her breath as the picture began to form in her mind's eye.

Someone had paid Boyd to make those calls.

Someone had put him up to it.

The same way someone had paid a man to dump the bodies. Someone who liked to manipulate from behind closed doors, but never wanted to stick his neck out.

Rachel could feel her pulse quickening, and she set her teeth together tightly.

The man in their interrogation room wasn't subtle. Wasn't clever. Wasn't sly.

He'd run from the cops and slammed into a barrier.

No… he was just another pawn.

She stared at the transaction details.

She needed it traced. To find out who'd wired the thousand dollars.

She placed a call, tapping her foot as the phone rang.

"Come on, come on," she muttered to herself, standing isolated in the evidence room.

Finally, a voice answered on the other end of the line. "IT department, how can I assist you?"

"Hi, this is Ranger Rachel Blackwood. I need to trace a transaction made through a cash app."

"Sure thing, Ranger. Can I get the details?"

Rachel read off the account information, tapping her foot impatiently against the floor.

Who could have paid Boyd to make those calls?

"Doesn't seem to go anywhere," the voice said.

"Come again?"

"The cash was sent from a dummy account. Only a couple minor transactions."

Rachel frowned. "What were the other transactions?"

"Nothing much. A pair of shoes. A watch."

Rachel was pacing now, feeling her frustration mounting. "What type of shoes?" she said at last.

"Umm… Hang on."

The sound of clicking resonated in the background. Then came the reply. "Men's dress shoes. Brown leather. A strange little golden swoop on the side."

Rachel's jaw dropped. "You're sure?"

"Yeah. Sorry I couldn't be of more help."

"No. No, it's fine."

Rachel lowered her phone, her brow furrowing. She then turned to the stairs and marched back up, moving swiftly.

Those shoes…

She'd spotted them.

She felt sure she had.

But maybe it was just a mistake. A trick of a desperate mind.

Time was running out, and the killer was still in the wind.

CHAPTER THIRTY ONE

Rain lashed against the windowpane, obscuring Rachel's view of the parked car outside the precinct. She leaned closer, her breath fogging up the glass as she watched the lawyer climb back into the vehicle. The driver moved around the side of the car with a briskness that caught her attention.

"Come on, buddy," she murmured to herself, her deep brown eyes narrowing in suspicion. Her fingers traced the rim of her hat, a comforting habit.

But her eyes were like those of a hawk, fixed on the man's shoes.

She'd spotted them as the lawyer entered the interrogation room.

And now, as she stared, she felt a faint shiver down her spine.

The driver's shoes came into focus as he stepped under a streetlamp. Rachel peered closer through the rain-streaked window. Brown leather with a golden emblem on the side—a match for the killer's credit card purchase.

A surge of adrenaline coursed through her veins, her heart pounding like thunder in her ears.

The driver was already closing the door for the lawyer. He was moving fast.

"Damn it!" she hissed, pushing away from the window. Her worn-in boots pounded against the floor as she sprinted toward the exit.

She stepped out under the rain-streaked sky, hurrying down the steps. Droplets struck her skin like cold pebbles. She blinked away the water, taking the steps outside the precinct two at a time.

"Hey!" she shouted as she closed in on the car, heart hammering wildly in her chest. "Get out of the car! Now!"

But the driver didn't seem to hear her. Or maybe he did, and chose to ignore her warning. His brake lights were on, but the engine was grumbling. And suddenly, the car began to move, turning out of the parking lot.

Rachel sprinted toward her own waiting car, remote starting the engine.

She flung herself into the front seat and began to follow the fleeing vehicle.

But it moved slowly. Perhaps he hadn't heard her…

No… no, he seemed not to have noticed her.

She frowned, keeping to the road as raindrops picked up, pouring in sheets from the sky.

The rain came down in heavy bursts, a relentless torrent that seemed to swallow the world whole. Each droplet struck the windshield like a bullet, and the wipers fought valiantly against them, but the darkness was nearly impenetrable. The narrow road twisted and turned, flanked by dense ravines on either side, which cast eerie shadows that danced across the asphalt as lightning tore through the sky.

Rachel gripped the steering wheel tightly, her knuckles turning white. Her heart thundered in her chest almost as loudly as the storm outside. She squinted through the downpour, straining to keep the car ahead in her sights. It was him; she was sure of it. If she lost him now, there might never be another chance.

As the car in front of her sped up, Rachel pressed harder on the accelerator. She could feel the engine's growl reverberate through her entire body, a living, breathing thing with an insatiable hunger for speed. The distance between them closed, but she knew better than to get too close. Instead, she weaved in and out of the few other cars on the road, using them as cover to maintain a safe distance.

Thomas would be proud, Rachel thought, recalling the countless late-night training sessions with her mentor, Thomas Greywolf. He had taught her everything he knew about evasive maneuvers, pursuit tactics, and the subtle art of remaining unseen even when you were right under someone's nose.

A sudden flash of lightning illuminated the road ahead, and Rachel's heart skipped a beat as she saw the car swerve dangerously close to the edge. It was an opportunity she couldn't pass up. With a deep breath, she pushed the pedal further, her pulse racing in time with the engine.

"Come on," she urged herself, "you've got this."

As the distance between them shrank, Rachel could feel her resolve hardening like steel.

As Rachel closed the gap between her and the suspect's car, the rain continued to fall in heavy sheets, creating a symphony of droplets against the windshield. The wipers struggled to keep up with the onslaught, but she remained undeterred as she focused on the vehicle ahead.

Through the blurry curtain of water, she could finally make out the details of the license plate: New Mexico—Land of Enchantment. Not a Texas plate. Strange. The numbers were partially obscured by mud, but she managed to discern the last four digits, "7H23."

"Got you," she whispered, her voice barely audible over the sound of the rain and the engine.

As the suspect's car swerved around a bend, Rachel noticed something that sent a chill down her spine.

With each passing mile, Rachel's determination grew stronger. The rain continued to pour, and she fought to maintain control of her vehicle as it hydroplaned across the slick asphalt, but she refused to falter. Her thoughts raced with a mixture of strategy and resolve, as she envisioned finally confronting the killer face-to-face. The enormity of the task before her loomed like a specter in the darkness, but she knew that she was ready.

The night sky roared with fury as lightning split the darkness, casting jagged bolts across the horizon. The thunder that followed shook Rachel to her core, a deep rumble reverberating through her bones. Blinding flashes illuminated the torrential rain, turning the world into a chaotic symphony of light and sound.

"Damn it," Rachel muttered under her breath, her knuckles white on the steering wheel. The suspect's taillights flickered in and out of view, a sinister red glow in the blackness. Her heart pounded in her chest, adrenaline coursing through her veins. She couldn't lose him now, not after everything she'd risked.

Another brilliant flash of lightning seared across the sky, momentarily blinding her. Rachel blinked away the afterimage, squinting in an attempt to regain her focus on the road. In that instant, her car hit a deep puddle, sending her into a sudden, heart-stopping spin.

"Shit!" she cried out as her hands fought for control of the wheel. The world outside her window blurred into a dizzying whirlwind of darkness and rain. Panic clawed at her insides, threatening to consume her entirely. "You can regain control!"

Rachel gritted her teeth, forcing herself to ease off the accelerator, and turned the wheel, her heart hammering in her chest as she fought against the terrifying loss of control. Inch by agonizing inch, her car began to straighten, her tires finally gripping the slick road once more.

With her car back under control, Rachel's eyes darted frantically from side to side, searching for any sign of the vehicle she'd been pursuing. The rain had only intensified, making visibility nearly impossible. Her heart raced in her chest and doubt began to creep into her mind.

"Where are you?" she muttered under her breath, her grip tightening on the wheel. "I can't lose you now."

As Rachel pressed onward, a faint light flickered in the distance. Squinting through the blur of rainwater streaming down her windshield, she could barely make out the neon sign of a run-down diner tucked away off the main road. The building was small and weather-beaten, with peeling paint and an air of abandonment. Faded letters adorning the roof spelled out "Marty's Diner," the name barely visible through the storm.

As Rachel pulled into the nearly empty gravel parking lot, she noticed the other car tucked away near the rear of the diner, its license plate matching the one she'd been chasing. A jolt of adrenaline surged through her, and she clenched her fists in anticipation.

As she sat in her car, the rain pounding against the roof like a relentless drumbeat, Rachel wrestled with her decision.

Wait for backup?

Ethan would be tracking her GPS. He'd be on the way.

But… who knew how long that would take?

The rain intensified, each droplet pelting the windshield like a barrage of tiny bullets. The torrential downpour transformed the parking lot into a shallow lake, the surface marred by countless ripples and splashes. Rachel's nose tingled with the sharp scent of damp earth as it permeated the car's interior.

As she scanned the diner for any signs of movement, a flash of lightning illuminated the scene, casting eerie shadows across the wet pavement. Rachel's eyes flickered back to the parked car, her breath catching in her throat as she noticed the faint glint of metal near the driver's side door.

She hesitated for only a moment before making up her mind. Rachel unbuckled her seatbelt and slid out of the car, her shoes sinking into the waterlogged gravel. She moved stealthily, her body low and her senses heightened, as she approached the suspect's vehicle.

As she drew closer, her heart raced at the thought of finally apprehending the killer. The weight of her gun, secure in her hand, offered her a small comfort.

Her eyes narrowed, her resolve strengthening like treated iron.

She approached the car, gun rising slowly, aiming at the door.

As she cautiously approached the driver's side door. The rain soaked her to the bone, but she barely noticed, her focus solely on the car. She gripped the handle and yanked the door open.

She froze.

Only one figure sat in the car.

The lawyer.

The woman, sitting in the back seat, had her hand up, clutching at her neck, her eyes wide. The self-assured, confident, and cutthroat professional from the interrogation room was gone.

Only fear remained.

"Help me," the lawyer gasped, her hand clamped tightly around her neck, desperation clouding her eyes.

She was bleeding.

Rivulets seeped around her fingers, down her hand.

Blood poured down her neck from where she'd been cut.

Rachel's mind moved rapidly. "Keep pressure applied!" she directed.

And at the same time, she peered into the front seat. The keys were in the ignition.

But the driver was gone. He must have spotted her.

As she returned her attention to the lawyer and opened her mouth to speak, she heard a sudden flutter of movement.

Thumping footsteps.

She half turned.

Too late.

Suddenly, a searing pain exploded at the back of her head, and Rachel's vision went dark. Her legs gave out beneath her, and she crashed to the ground, the cold rainwater soaking through her clothes. The last thing she heard before losing consciousness was the thud of her head hitting the pavement.

CHAPTER THIRTY TWO

She was woken, her head throbbing, by the jostle of the moving vehicle. She blinked, white-hot lances of pain shooting through her skull. The relentless hum of the car's engine filled Rachel's ears as she sat in the backseat, her hands bound tightly in front of her. The worn leather beneath her seemed to echo the groans of the victims who had been here before her. Her heart pounded against her chest, each beat whispering a silent prayer for survival.

"Can't you see?" the killer was saying, his voice tinged with both arrogance and sadness. "I'm saving the world, Rachel. I have to do this."

His words were like icy daggers in the stifling heat of the Texas sun. The rain had vanished, it was daylight, and now the bright sun beamed through the windows.

At her side, she felt a warm body shift. She blinked again, ignoring the pain, and glanced over to see the lawyer was recovering as well.

The woman was holding a bloody rag to her throat. Her eyes kept fluttering, and the loss of blood was clearly taxing her.

Rachel felt shivers running down her spine despite the stale warmth of the car.

"Feeding the earth in the oil fields, it's my destiny," he continued, his eyes fixed firmly on the road ahead. "These women become one with the land, giving life to the black gold that sustains us all."

Rachel clenched her teeth, anger and fear mingling together in a storm within her. Glancing at the rearview mirror, she met his gaze for a moment.

He sighed, almost mournfully. "I know how it must look to you, but I promise, this is my purpose. It's a necessary evil."

As they sped along the dusty roads, surrounded by the sprawling expanse of the barren landscape, Rachel couldn't help but think of Aunt Sarah. The only family she really had left. Her aunt blamed her for the failure to solve her parents' case.

And now…

Rachel might never get the chance to make it right.

The killer's expression flickered with something akin to regret, but his conviction remained unshaken. "I wish it didn't have to be this way," he murmured, his voice barely audible above the drone of the engine. "But I must continue my work."

As they drove further into the desolate wasteland, Rachel knew she was running out of time. If she couldn't find a way to break free and overcome this madman, she would become just another forgotten soul in the unforgiving embrace of the oil fields.

She could feel the lawyer shifting again at her side. Neither of them had much time left.

Rachel's breathing grew shallow as she glanced over at the lawyer, her battered body slumped against the car door. The woman's eyes were glazed with pain, the blood-soaked rag still pressed against her throat. Rachel could only imagine the agony she was experiencing.

"Can you… remember who you've taken?" Rachel asked the killer, trying to keep him engaged in conversation while subtly maneuvering her bound hands toward the brim of her hat.

"Of course," he replied, his voice tinged with sorrow and a hint of pride. "Each one was special. Each one had a purpose."

"Tell me about them," Rachel urged, her fingers finally reaching the feather tucked into the hatband—a small memento, adorned with a hidden metal nub.

She pulled the feather free, hiding it along the length of her wrist as she lowered her hands again.

His eyes glanced in the mirror, like searchlights, but missed the motion.

He was still too drunk on the sound of his own voice.

With every word he spoke, she carefully sawed at the ropes binding her wrists, the sharp edge gradually fraying the fibers.

The landscape outside the car began to shift. Distant silhouettes of machinery rose against the horizon like mechanical monsters, heralding their approach to an oil field. Rachel's breath hitched; she knew what awaited her there—death, darkness, and an eternity buried beneath the earth.

"I'm sorry I have to do this to you," he said, his voice trembling with emotion. "But it's for the greater good."

With a final, desperate tug, the rope snapped apart, freeing her hands. She steadied her breathing, strategizing her next move. She needed to act fast, catch him off guard. And above all, she needed to survive.

The car jolted to a stop, sending clouds of dust billowing around them. The harsh sunlight outlined the desolate landscape, casting long shadows across the barren desert floor. Rachel's heart pounded in her chest as she glanced around, searching for any signs of civilization or help. There was nothing but endless stretches of sun-scorched earth and the occasional skeletal remains of a long-dead tree.

"Here we are," the killer said softly, his voice barely audible over the sound of the idling engine. "I'm so sorry for this."

He had such plain features. Eyes that might've been described as kind in any other setting.

Rachel clenched her fists, feeling the sweat on her palms mix with the dirt from the torn ropes. She took a deep breath, steadying herself for the confrontation that would follow.

As the killer stepped out of the car and circled around to the back door, Rachel braced herself against the seat, her muscles coiled like a spring. The door creaked open, revealing his silhouette framed by the merciless sun.

"Please try to understand," he whispered, reaching for her.

"Understand this," Rachel hissed, lunging forward. Her body slammed into his, driven by the force of pure adrenaline.

She struck him with the full force of her small frame. They hit the ground hard. The breath was knocked from her lungs.

She tried to scramble on top, but he was bucking desperately.

"Stop!" the killer shouted, struggling to break free from Rachel's unyielding grip. "You don't know what you're—"

They tumbled along the ground, a tangle of limbs and desperation, until suddenly, Rachel felt the ground shift under her.

An incline.

Her hand was at his throat, but he was trying to gouge at her eyes.

The two of them began rolling down the incline as they thrashed about, kicking up dust.

CHAPTER THIRTY THREE

Rachel grappled, her hands straining, her breath coming in quick bursts. Sand got into her mouth, and she spat.

Rachel and the killer tumbled down the incline, picking up speed as they rolled.

Her shoulder struck a rock, and she cried out in pain. The killer's grip on her loosened, and she took advantage, regaining the upper position.

But they continued to tumble, rolling along the ground with the change in motion.

At the base of the incline, the two of them came to a sudden halt, if only for a brief moment.

Rachel's arms strained, but he had caught her wrists, holding her.

And in that moment, they remained motionless.

The desert stretched out before them like an endless, desolate ocean. The tall cactuses that surrounded Rachel and the killer stood sentinel in the arid wasteland, their imposing silhouettes casting long shadows. The air was thick with tension as the two combatants struggled in the dust, a deadly dance.

Where she pinned him, her muscles trembled from exertion as she fought to subdue him. She could feel the sweat pouring down her face, stinging her eyes. The grit of sand and dust filled her nostrils and mouth as they rolled in the dirt, but she didn't care. All that mattered was taking this monster down, once and for all.

The killer's face contorted in rage, his eyes wild with hatred. He tried to buck her off, but Rachel held firm.

She focused on her breathing—slow and steady—just as Aunt Sarah had taught her during their many hunting trips together.

The sun bathed the desert in a bright glow as Rachel's and the killer's labored breaths punctuated the otherwise silent morning. The soft crunch of sand beneath their struggling bodies mingled with the low growls of exertion, adding to the tense atmosphere. Rachel's muscles strained against the killer's strength, her grip tightening around his wrists as she fought to keep him pinned down.

The shadows cast by the towering cactuses danced and shifted as they grappled, heightening the sense of urgency that pulsed through Rachel's veins. A bead of sweat trickled down her forehead, stinging her eyes as she blinked it away. She could feel the quickening rhythm of her own heartbeat, a drumbeat urging her on.

The killer's face contorted, and he suddenly managed to break one hand free from her grasp. He swung at her wildly, but Rachel dodged his attack. She gritted her teeth, refusing to give in to fear or distraction.

"Stupid girl!" the killer screamed, his voice harsh and venomous. "You think you can stop me? You're just like the rest of them… weak!"

Rachel's jaw tightened, but she remained steadfast, searching for an opening to strike.

Anger bubbled within Rachel, but she clamped down on it, knowing that letting emotions take control would be her downfall. She focused on her breathing, steadying herself as she prepared for the next move.

Suddenly, she heard the sound of scraping metal.

His hand had dropped, and she spotted where he pulled a knife from his waistband.

The sun glinted off the killer's hunting knife, casting an ominous streak of light on his twisted face as tried to stab upwards, off his back.

This forced her to make a split-second decision. Rather than risking injury, she released her grip and pushed back.

They both regained their feet rapidly, gasping and sweaty.

Rachel shot a temporary glance back toward the vehicle at the top of the incline.

The lawyer was still in there, bleeding from her neck.

Alive, for now. Rachel remembered with the other victims that they'd had superficial cuts. This man knew how to hurt his victims without killing them. A horrifying thought.

Rachel returned her attention to the knife-wielding maniac.

He stood glaring at her, teeth bared. He kept glancing at the sky, as if fearful it might fall on him at any moment.

"You don't know what you're doing," he whispered.

She swallowed, stepping back, keeping her distance. "You like the shadows, don't you?" she whispered.

He moved to the left. She followed. He moved to the right. She countered.

"You hired someone to hide the bodies. Hired someone to place a phone call. And all the while, you're sneaking around. Well, I see you now!" she said, her voice hoarse. "I *see* you."

She glared at him, refusing to look away.

He quailed under her stare and fidgeted uncomfortably, clutching tightly at the knife.

"You don't have to do this," she said.

He snarled and lunged forward.

Rachel sidestepped and kicked his wrist. The knife clattered to the ground, and he stumbled.

She grabbed the knife and held it to his throat.

"Don't move," she said, her voice trembling.

He froze, and for a moment, the only sound was the wind rustling through the cacti.

"Now," Rachel said, her voice steady. "Let's talk about what you did."

He tensed.

There was a sudden shout behind her. A strangled noise. The woman in the car, pleading for help.

Rachel instinctively glanced back, and the killer jammed his elbow into her gut.

She let out a gasp of air, and he tore the knife away from her.

Her own compassion, fear on behalf of the bleeding woman, nearly cost her her own life.

The knife came whistling toward her neck, but she dodged it again.

She used her agility to evade his thrusts and punches, countering with swift blows of her own. As they circled one another, Rachel searched for any opportunity to exploit his weaknesses.

The killer's face was twisted into a furious expression, like a grotesque Halloween mask.

His timid, almost apologetic nature had vanished to be replaced by something feral.

"You're going to cost the world everything!" he was saying, his voice rising. "The oil… it's the blood of the earth! It has to be fed!"

He swiped at her, his crazed rantings becoming shrill with the motion.

She lunged back, avoiding the blow, but feeling the breeze of his arm lashing through the air.

She wasn't a talkative sort, so she didn't point out how insane he sounded.

But if he was talking, he was exhausting himself. So she said, conserving her own breath with short words, "The earth needs to be fed?"

He blinked, staring at her, his knife waving back and forth where he stood, watching her attentively, his body lithe like a snake's.

"Yes!" he said, pausing if only for the moment. He met her gaze, an eagerness to his eyes, as if he thought he might be able to *reach* her with his madness.

"The earth needs the oil! It's the only thing that gives it the power to live and sustain itself! Without it, we will all die!"

Rachel stared back at him, feeling a chill run down her spine.

He seemed to deflate before her, his shoulders slumping.

Rachel watched him, her heart briefly twinging for the pain and sorrow that she saw in his eyes.

He was like a wild beast.

The knife like a claw, talon, or tooth.

She'd faced predators in the wilderness before. This was no different. Hunter vs. prey.

Sometimes, the biggest predators were startled by the smallest of creatures.

In the wild, creatures would often make themselves appear larger. The change in size startling the more dangerous aggressor.

He was staring at her, a mad glint to his gaze.

She met the glare, her eyes hooded, her hands tense at her sides.

"I feed the land," he whispered. "Someone has to. Like my father. I feed it. What do you do? Hmm? What do you do!" His voice screeched like the call of a vulture.

She just kept her gaze on him, saying nothing.

He was pacing back and forth now, clearly agitated, shaking his head side to side.

She watched him closely, tense, patient, her eyes never leaving the knife.

And then he lunged.

She didn't hesitate. She'd seen his legs coiling, seen his muscles tense.

Instead of backing away, though, she flung her arms *out.*

A distraction. Making her frame larger.

He hesitated only briefly, and she went low.

Her hands had gone *up*, and his knife had followed, and then she'd dove *under* the blade.

She caught him around the legs, hearing the knife clatter as it fell from his hand due to the impact.

She slammed him into a cactus, and he let out a scream of pain as the prickles jabbed at him.

Rachel stood up and backed away, watching as the killer struggled to disentangle himself from the cactus. He was bleeding from multiple scratches and pricks, but he no longer seemed to feel the pain. Instead, his eyes were fixed on her, burning with a hatred that chilled her to the bone.

"You think you've won?" he snarled, his voice hoarse from the exertion. "You're nothing! You're just a weak little girl!"

Rachel felt a surge of anger rise within her, but she forced it down. She knew that getting emotional would only lead to mistakes. Instead, she kept her eyes locked on his, waiting for him to make a move.

The killer pushed himself up from the cactus and lunged at her once again. Rachel sidestepped his attack and delivered a powerful punch to his stomach. He doubled over, gasping for air, and she took the opportunity to deliver a swift kick to his face.

The killer fell to the ground, his head hitting the sand with a sickening thud. Rachel stood over him, panting heavily, her hands balled into fists.

The killer groaned and tried to push himself up, but Rachel kicked him in the ribs, sending him sprawling back onto the ground.

"You're done," she said, her voice low and steady. "Give up now, and I won't hurt you anymore."

The killer glared up at her, his eyes filled with hatred and defiance.

"You're making a mistake," he said, his voice hoarse. "You don't know this land like I do."

Rachel shook her head. "No," she said. "I know it well enough. And I know that you're done."

The killer snarled and tried to get up, but Rachel pushed him back down with her boot. "I said, you're done."

He lay there, panting and glaring up at her. After a few moments, his defiance melted away, replaced by a look of resignation.

Rachel stepped back, letting out a breath she hadn't realized she'd been holding.

He then tried to surge upward one last time.

But she'd been expecting this.

She struck him a final time, and he slumped back to the ground.

She stood over him, gasping under the sun, feeling like a wolf with cornered prey.

Then she glanced sharply back at the car.

The lawyer was still bleeding out.

"I'm coming!" she called out, gasping. "Hang on!"

She turned on her heel, moving fast up the incline, scrambling along the dusty ground.

Behind her, she heard the killer's labored breathing, but she didn't look back.

She reached the vehicle. The lawyer was still alive, but barely. The woman's head lolled to the side, and a pale hand held a rag to her bloody neck.

She cursed, glancing over her shoulder toward where the killer lay motionless.

A decision had to be made.

The lawyer was going to bleed out.

But she needed to secure the killer.

Dragging him back up the incline, though, would take too long.

She didn't have her handcuffs with her.

Shit.

No time to dawdle.

Think. She had to…

She bit her lip and then swung back out of the car, sprinting back down the incline.

He was groaning as she reached him and began tugging at his pants.

"What the hell…" he mumbled into the dust.

She removed his pants and then used his discarded knife to cut them lengthwise.

Then, with two makeshift ropes, she used the pants to tie his arms around one of the cactuses. She slammed her foot against the needles, breaking them or indenting them to prevent them from harming him.

He spluttered and protested as she worked, moving fast.

All the while, she thought of the lawyer, bleeding out on the top of the incline.

Come on. Hurry… Hurry, her subconscious nagged at her.

Finally, she was done.

The killer was tied up, unable to move.

She glanced up at the incline one last time, her heart pounding. And then she sprinted back up the dirt path, back to the car.

The lawyer was still alive, but barely.

Rachel grabbed the rag and pressed it against the woman's neck, applying pressure.

The lawyer groaned in response, but Rachel said, "You need to stay awake. Hear me? Stay awake! Apply pressure."

The lawyer's hand moved up, trembling, touching the makeshift bandage. She was coherent enough to follow instructions, at least.

Rachel breathed out a sigh of relief, but she knew they couldn't stay there for long. They needed medical attention and fast. She quickly searched the car, finding a first aid kit and some water bottles. She poured some water onto the rag and pressed it against the lawyer's wound, trying to clean it as best she could. The woman winced in pain but didn't move away.

"We need to get out of here," Rachel said, her voice urgent. "Can you sit up front?"

The lawyer shook her head weakly. "I don't think so," she said, her voice barely audible.

Rachel cursed under her breath. She had to think of something fast. She looked around, trying to find any signs of civilization. But they were in the middle of nowhere, with nothing but sand and cactuses as far as the eye could see.

Rachel moved back around the car, hastening to the driver's side. She shot a final look down the incline toward where the killer was slumped by the cactus, and then she gunned the engine.

They needed to make it to the hospital before the lawyer bled out.

As they drove, Rachel could feel the woman's life slipping away. She didn't know if they were going to make it in time. She pushed the car as fast as it would go, her hands gripping the steering wheel tightly.

The lawyer was barely conscious, her eyes closed and her breathing shallow. Rachel kept talking to her, trying to keep her awake.

"You're going to make it," she said, her voice shaking. "Just hang on a little longer. We're almost there."

But the lawyer didn't respond. Rachel could feel her own panic rising, but she forced it down. She had to stay focused on driving.

She hadn't been able to save the others.

Hadn't been able to save her parents.

More blood… An image flashed through her mind of a shattered window. Bloodstains on the glass.

She pushed aside thoughts of that night, flooring the pedal and tearing up the road in search of some vindication.

CHAPTER THIRTY FOUR

The drive to the hospital was a blur for Rachel. She kept one hand on the wheel and the other twisted awkwardly and extended into the back seat, her hand pressed hard against the lawyer's neck, trying to stem the flow of blood. Every time the woman groaned or moved, Rachel pressed harder, her heart pounding in her chest.

After what seemed like an eternity, they pulled up to the hospital, tires squealing against the asphalt of the roundabout. Rachel practically dragged the victim out of the car and into the emergency room, shouting for help. Doctors and nurses swarmed around them, taking the woman from Rachel's grasp and rushing her into surgery. Rachel stood in the hallway, shaking and covered in blood, watching as the doors to the OR swung shut.

She closed her eyes, breathing heavily, and slumped against the wall. Her eyes closed.

She pulled out her phone with shaking fingers and sent a text.

Suspect located at following coordinates. Apprehend now*! Look for a cactus.*

She sent the message, then sent the data from her GPS.

She watched as the message sent, and then swiped with weary fingers on the phone.

She lowered herself onto a bench outside the OR, facing a vending machine, her eyes fluttering, wanting to close, wanting to find the sweet assuaging of sleep.

But her own curiosity carried her forward.

With a start, she realized she didn't even know the name of the man she'd fought in the desert.

She logged into the database and cycled to employee records.

She entered the lawyer's information, and then scanned the details on her chauffeur.

She blinked.

A smiling face stared back from the image. The name under the image read "Tyler Dobson."

"Hello, Tyler," she murmured.

She recognized the man, though in the desert, she'd grappled with a more haggard version of the face staring back at her.

Rachel's heart rate increased as she read through Tyler's file. He had been working for the law firm for over five years, and there were no previous incidents or complaints against him. It appeared he was a model employee.

She closed her eyes, hanging her head briefly.

And then she stood up.

Exhaustion weighed on her, but this wasn't over. The killer was still free.

And a man like that belonged in a cage.

She began walking down the slick, tiled hall of the hospital. Sleep was an elusive promise now. She moved swiftly, fishing keys from her pocket.

She made her way outside, the cool morning air hitting her face, and jogged to the car. She got in, started the engine, and headed toward the coordinates she had sent earlier.

As she drove, she kept glancing at the phone on her seat next to her.

Pieces were slowly fitting together.

Dobson's father had been involved with a fringe environmentalist group. Dobson had been raised by his father until the man's death fifteen years ago.

Working on an oil rig. Routine maintenance, and a tragic accident.

She stared at the image of Tyler's smiling face.

It didn't seem right.

None of this felt right.

And women were dead.

She drove rapidly, moving swiftly to the rendezvous with Ethan at the suspect's location.

And then her phone vibrated. She glanced down. A message from Ethan Morgan.

On it. Found him. Where are you?

Found him.

She let out a long sigh of relief.

Custody? she wrote back.

Affirmative, came the quick reply.

And only then did she stop, slowly driving off to the shoulder of the road, her eyes heavy, exhaustion weighing on her.

She put the car in park, idling in the morning light.

Her eyes kept drooping.

She was so damn tired.

And as her head dipped, the thought of driving back to a motel seemed… unlikely at best. A hassle at worst.

No…

No, these seats were perfectly comfortable.

Her mind began to drift… and darkness closed in, even as the engine rumbled.

CHAPTER THIRTY FIVE

Rachel woke to someone knocking on the parked car's window. She blinked sleep from her eyes, trying to regain her senses.

She blinked and looked up, noticing a figure peering through the window.

She reached out, trying to roll down the window. But it was stuck.

She frowned, glanced with a shaky gaze toward the dash.

"Shit."

The car had run out of gas, idling for who knew how long.

She blinked a few times, rubbing the sleep from her eyes, and then slowly pushed open the door.

The tall, smiling frame of Ethan Morgan stood out against the backdrop of sunlight.

"Howdy, partner," he said, his southern drawl even more pronounced than usual.

"Ethan," she muttered, giving a quick nod.

She leaned back, reclining her head against the seat and trying to catch her bearings.

Suddenly she looked sharply at him. "You get him in custody?"

"Mhmm. Booked him a few hours ago. Been looking for you since. Your phone's dead."

"Yeah. Car's dead too."

Ethan leaned with one arm against the roof of the car, surveying her where she sat in the front seat.

She didn't like this position. His shadow swelled over her. And while she liked Ethan, she didn't know him yet.

Trust was earned. And earning took time.

She slipped out of the front seat, inhaling the cool, Texas air on the side of the abandoned road.

Rachel's eyes scanned the surroundings, taking note of the spiky cacti and rocky hills. She felt a sense of relief that they had finally caught the killer, but her mind was still racing with questions.

"What do we know about Tyler Dobson?" she asked, breaking the silence.

"He's a chauffeur at the firm, seemed like a pretty average guy. We did a background check on him, but nothing really stood out," Ethan replied, his eyes scanning the area as well.

Rachel frowned, still not convinced. "But why would a driver suddenly start killing women?"

Ethan shrugged. "Six arrests on his old man. Child endangerment."

"What?"

"His old man used to make Tyler run his night shifts."

Rachel frowned.

Ethan looked off into the distance, his brow furrowed. There was something in his eyes that made Rachel think this was personal to him. He murmured, "His old man would drink. Have the kid man the controls. Apparently told his kid the world would end if he didn't do a good job. Some shit like that."

"Well…"

"Yeah. Well."

The two of them leaned against the car now, both staring off into the distance, both lost in their own thoughts.

Rachel then shrugged. "I need a ride. And a tow for this car. My car is back at some abandoned diner."

"Mhmm. Already called a truck."

She flashed him one of her rare smiles, adjusted her hat, and then began moving back toward the SUV idling on the side of the road ahead of her.

Ethan fell into step a second later.

A case solved.

But another case… lodged in the back of her mind… kept haunting her, like a spirit that wouldn't leave her side.

Her aunt's words kept echoing.

The blame resting squarely on Rachel's shoulders. She hadn't solved the case.

She frowned, her smile fading once more as she approached the waiting car.

EPILOGUE

Rachel stood in the middle of her small, sparsely furnished apartment, her eyes darting from one bare wall to another. The space was a reflection of her own life—minimal and functional, devoid of unnecessary distractions. The only luxury in her otherwise austere surroundings was an impressive collection of weapons displayed on a meticulously maintained rack. Each of the weapons used to hunt some creature over the years.

And yet she stood there, motionless, eyeing a rifle she'd once used to hunt a three-hundred-pound mountain lion.

She could not shake off her aunt Sarah's words from their last encounter. The blame and disappointment that weighed heavily on Rachel's shoulders seemed to seep into every corner of the room, casting shadows on the vibrant patterns of the single woven tapestry that adorned her bed. She closed her eyes and took a deep breath, attempting to ground herself amidst the emotional turmoil.

"Focus," she muttered under her breath.

She paced back and forth, her boots echoing against the wooden floor, replaying the events leading up to this crucial moment in her mind. As she sifted through the information, she felt the pieces finally click into place like the tumblers of a lock aligning.

But they never fully aligned.

A piece was missing.

Had always been missing.

In her pursuit, she had only ever focused solely on the tangible evidence left behind at the crime scene—the bloodstains, the shattered window, the scattered belongings. But it was what wasn't there that held the key to solving the case. The absence of her parents' bodies, the lack of any witnesses, and the eerie silence that had lingered in the air like a dense fog. It was as if they had vanished without a trace.

So*mething…or someone deliberately concealed these details,* she thought, her hands clenched into fists as anger bubbled within her.

Her room was dimly lit, casting shadows that danced in the corners as the last rays of sunlight fought their way through the small, dusty window.

Her parents had disappeared. Assumed murdered.

By who, though?

And who had hidden the clues?

Someone…

Who knew what law enforcement would look for?

Someone on the inside?

She felt a cold chill go down her spine.

Frowning, she turned and approached her laptop on the slim, round kitchen table.

She opened the laptop, took in a steady, shaking breath. But then she summoned resolve. Summoned the disapproval in her aunt's voice.

She would see this through.

Her parents deserved it. An abandoned room. A shattered window… bloodstains on the glass. It all came back to her, haunting her. She could remember ten-year-old Rachel trembling, shaking horribly.

That same feeling of *knowing* deep in her gut that something terrible had happened.

She was a tracker, after all.

A hunter.

It was time to find out who'd killed her parents.

NOW AVAILABLE!

NOT THIS TIME
(A Rachel Blackwood Suspense Thriller—Book Two)

Texas Ranger (and part Native American) Rachel Blackwood, fierce and resilient, must cross the harsh Texas landscape while tracking the most notorious serial killers. When a historic ranch is rattled by a series of chilling murders, Rachel is plunged deep into the world of rodeos and ranching, racing to uncover dark secrets before the killer strikes again…

"A masterpiece of thriller and mystery."
—Books and Movie Reviews, Roberto Mattos (re Once Gone)

NOT THIS TIME (A Rachel Blackwood Suspense Thriller—Book 2) is Book #2 in a long-anticipated new series by #1 bestseller and USA Today bestselling author Blake Pierce, whose bestseller *The Perfect Wife* (a free download) has received over 20,000 five star reviews.

As a child, Rachel felt a connection to her Native American heritage, learning traditional customs and survival skills from the aunt who raised her. Haunted for years by her parents' mysterious and unsolved deaths, Rachel vowed to find their killer—and protect all other innocent lives from the same fate.

Can Rachel find the killer in time before he strikes again?

A page-turning and harrowing suspense thriller featuring a brilliant and tortured protagonist, the RACHEL BLACKWOOD series is a riveting mystery, packed with suspense, twists and turns, revelations, and driven by a breakneck pace that will keep you flipping pages late into the night.

Future books in the series are also available.

"An edge of your seat thriller in a new series that keeps you turning pages! ...So many twists, turns and red herrings… I can't wait to see what happens next."
—Reader review (Her Last Wish)

"A strong, complex story about two FBI agents trying to stop a serial killer. If you want an author to capture your attention and have you guessing, yet trying to put the pieces together, Pierce is your author!"
—Reader review (Her Last Wish)

"A typical Blake Pierce twisting, turning, roller coaster ride suspense thriller. Will have you turning the pages to the last sentence of the last chapter!!!"
—Reader review (City of Prey)

"Right from the start we have an unusual protagonist that I haven't seen done in this genre before. The action is nonstop… A very atmospheric novel that will keep you turning pages well into the wee hours."
—Reader review (City of Prey)

"Everything that I look for in a book… a great plot, interesting characters, and grabs your interest right away. The book moves along at a breakneck pace and stays that way until the end. Now on go I to book two!"
—Reader review (Girl, Alone)

"Exciting, heart pounding, edge of your seat book… a must read for mystery and suspense readers!"
—Reader review (Girl, Alone)

Blake Pierce

Blake Pierce is the USA Today bestselling author of the RILEY PAGE mystery series, which includes seventeen books. Blake Pierce is also the author of the MACKENZIE WHITE mystery series, comprising fourteen books; of the AVERY BLACK mystery series, comprising six books; of the KERI LOCKE mystery series, comprising five books; of the MAKING OF RILEY PAIGE mystery series, comprising six books; of the KATE WISE mystery series, comprising seven books; of the CHLOE FINE psychological suspense mystery, comprising six books; of the JESSIE HUNT psychological suspense thriller series, comprising thirty-five books (and counting); of the AU PAIR psychological suspense thriller series, comprising three books; of the ZOE PRIME mystery series, comprising six books; of the ADELE SHARP mystery series, comprising sixteen books, of the EUROPEAN VOYAGE cozy mystery series, comprising six books; of the LAURA FROST FBI suspense thriller, comprising eleven books; of the ELLA DARK FBI suspense thriller, comprising twenty-one books (and counting); of the A YEAR IN EUROPE cozy mystery series, comprising nine books, of the AVA GOLD mystery series, comprising six books; of the RACHEL GIFT mystery series, comprising thirteen books (and counting); of the VALERIE LAW mystery series, comprising nine books; of the PAIGE KING mystery series, comprising eight books; of the MAY MOORE mystery series, comprising eleven books; of the CORA SHIELDS mystery series, comprising eight books; of the NICKY LYONS mystery series, comprising eight books, of the CAMI LARK mystery series, comprising ten books; of the AMBER YOUNG mystery series, comprising seven books (and counting); of the DAISY FORTUNE mystery series, comprising five books; of the FIONA RED mystery series, comprising eleven books (and counting); of the FAITH BOLD mystery series, comprising eleven books (and counting); of the JULIETTE HART mystery series, comprising five books (and counting); of the MORGAN CROSS mystery series, comprising nine books (and counting); of the FINN WRIGHT mystery series, comprising five books (and counting); and of the new SHEILA STONE suspense thriller series, comprising five books (and counting).

An avid reader and lifelong fan of the mystery and thriller genres, Blake loves to hear from you, so please feel free to visit www.blakepierceauthor.com to learn more and stay in touch.

BOOKS BY BLAKE PIERCE

SHEILA STONE SUSPENSE THRILLER

SILENT GIRL (Book #1)
SILENT TRAIL (Book #2)
SILENT NIGHT (Book #3)
SILENT HOUSE (Book #4)
SILENT SCREAM (Book #5)

FINN WRIGHT MYSTERY SERIES

WHEN YOU'RE MINE (Book #1)
WHEN YOU'RE SAFE (Book #2)
WHEN YOU'RE CLOSE (Book #3)
WHEN YOU'RE SLEEPING (Book #4)
WHEN YOU'RE SANE (Book #5)

MORGAN CROSS MYSTERY SERIES

FOR YOU (Book #1)
FOR RAGE (Book #2)
FOR LUST (Book #3)
FOR WRATH (Book #4)
FOREVER (Book #5)
FOR US (Book #6)
FOR NOW (Book #7)
FOR ONCE (Book #8)
FOR ETERNITY (Book #9)

JULIETTE HART MYSTERY SERIES

NOTHING TO FEAR (Book #1)
NOTHING THERE (Book #2)
NOTHING WATCHING (Book #3)
NOTHING HIDING (Book #4)
NOTHING LEFT (Book #5)

FAITH BOLD MYSTERY SERIES

SO LONG (Book #1)
SO COLD (Book #2)

SO SCARED (Book #3)
SO NORMAL (Book #4)
SO FAR GONE (Book #5)
SO LOST (Book #6)
SO ALONE (Book #7)
SO FORGOTTEN (Book #8)
SO INSANE (Book #9)
SO SMITTEN (Book #10)
SO SIMPLE (Book #11)

FIONA RED MYSTERY SERIES
LET HER GO (Book #1)
LET HER BE (Book #2)
LET HER HOPE (Book #3)
LET HER WISH (Book #4)
LET HER LIVE (Book #5)
LET HER RUN (Book #6)
LET HER HIDE (Book #7)
LET HER BELIEVE (Book #8)
LET HER FORGET (Book #9)
LET HER TRY (Book #10)
LET HER PLAY (Book #11)

DAISY FORTUNE MYSTERY SERIES
NEED YOU (Book #1)
CLAIM YOU (Book #2)
CRAVE YOU (Book #3)
CHOOSE YOU (Book #4)
CHASE YOU (Book #5)

AMBER YOUNG MYSTERY SERIES
ABSENT PITY (Book #1)
ABSENT REMORSE (Book #2)
ABSENT FEELING (Book #3)
ABSENT MERCY (Book #4)
ABSENT REASON (Book #5)
ABSENT SANITY (Book #6)
ABSENT LIFE (Book #7)

CAMI LARK MYSTERY SERIES

JUST ME (Book #1)
JUST OUTSIDE (Book #2)
JUST RIGHT (Book #3)
JUST FORGET (Book #4)
JUST ONCE (Book #5)
JUST HIDE (Book #6)
JUST NOW (Book #7)
JUST HOPE (Book #8)
JUST LEAVE (Book #9)
JUST TONIGHT (Book #10)

NICKY LYONS MYSTERY SERIES
ALL MINE (Book #1)
ALL HIS (Book #2)
ALL HE SEES (Book #3)
ALL ALONE (Book #4)
ALL FOR ONE (Book #5)
ALL HE TAKES (Book #6)
ALL FOR ME (Book #7)
ALL IN (Book #8)

CORA SHIELDS MYSTERY SERIES
UNDONE (Book #1)
UNWANTED (Book #2)
UNHINGED (Book #3)
UNSAID (Book #4)
UNGLUED (Book #5)
UNSTABLE (Book #6)
UNKNOWN (Book #7)
UNAWARE (Book #8)

MAY MOORE SUSPENSE THRILLER
NEVER RUN (Book #1)
NEVER TELL (Book #2)
NEVER LIVE (Book #3)
NEVER HIDE (Book #4)
NEVER FORGIVE (Book #5)
NEVER AGAIN (Book #6)
NEVER LOOK BACK (Book #7)
NEVER FORGET (Book #8)

NEVER LET GO (Book #9)
NEVER PRETEND (Book #10)
NEVER HESITATE (Book #11)

PAIGE KING MYSTERY SERIES
THE GIRL HE PINED (Book #1)
THE GIRL HE CHOSE (Book #2)
THE GIRL HE TOOK (Book #3)
THE GIRL HE WISHED (Book #4)
THE GIRL HE CROWNED (Book #5)
THE GIRL HE WATCHED (Book #6)
THE GIRL HE WANTED (Book #7)
THE GIRL HE CLAIMED (Book #8)

VALERIE LAW MYSTERY SERIES
NO MERCY (Book #1)
NO PITY (Book #2)
NO FEAR (Book #3)
NO SLEEP (Book #4)
NO QUARTER (Book #5)
NO CHANCE (Book #6)
NO REFUGE (Book #7)
NO GRACE (Book #8)
NO ESCAPE (Book #9)

RACHEL GIFT MYSTERY SERIES
HER LAST WISH (Book #1)
HER LAST CHANCE (Book #2)
HER LAST HOPE (Book #3)
HER LAST FEAR (Book #4)
HER LAST CHOICE (Book #5)
HER LAST BREATH (Book #6)
HER LAST MISTAKE (Book #7)
HER LAST DESIRE (Book #8)
HER LAST REGRET (Book #9)
HER LAST HOUR (Book #10)
HER LAST SHOT (Book #11)
HER LAST PRAYER (Book #12)
HER LAST LIE (Book #13)

AVA GOLD MYSTERY SERIES
CITY OF PREY (Book #1)
CITY OF FEAR (Book #2)
CITY OF BONES (Book #3)
CITY OF GHOSTS (Book #4)
CITY OF DEATH (Book #5)
CITY OF VICE (Book #6)

A YEAR IN EUROPE
A MURDER IN PARIS (Book #1)
DEATH IN FLORENCE (Book #2)
VENGEANCE IN VIENNA (Book #3)
A FATALITY IN SPAIN (Book #4)

ELLA DARK FBI SUSPENSE THRILLER
GIRL, ALONE (Book #1)
GIRL, TAKEN (Book #2)
GIRL, HUNTED (Book #3)
GIRL, SILENCED (Book #4)
GIRL, VANISHED (Book 5)
GIRL ERASED (Book #6)
GIRL, FORSAKEN (Book #7)
GIRL, TRAPPED (Book #8)
GIRL, EXPENDABLE (Book #9)
GIRL, ESCAPED (Book #10)
GIRL, HIS (Book #11)
GIRL, LURED (Book #12)
GIRL, MISSING (Book #13)
GIRL, UNKNOWN (Book #14)
GIRL, DECEIVED (Book #15)
GIRL, FORLORN (Book #16)
GIRL, REMADE (Book #17)
GIRL, BETRAYED (Book #18)
GIRL, BOUND (Book #19)
GIRL, REFORMED (Book #20)
GIRL, REBORN (Book #21)

LAURA FROST FBI SUSPENSE THRILLER
ALREADY GONE (Book #1)
ALREADY SEEN (Book #2)

ALREADY TRAPPED (Book #3)
ALREADY MISSING (Book #4)
ALREADY DEAD (Book #5)
ALREADY TAKEN (Book #6)
ALREADY CHOSEN (Book #7)
ALREADY LOST (Book #8)
ALREADY HIS (Book #9)
ALREADY LURED (Book #10)
ALREADY COLD (Book #11)

EUROPEAN VOYAGE COZY MYSTERY SERIES
MURDER (AND BAKLAVA) (Book #1)
DEATH (AND APPLE STRUDEL) (Book #2)
CRIME (AND LAGER) (Book #3)
MISFORTUNE (AND GOUDA) (Book #4)
CALAMITY (AND A DANISH) (Book #5)
MAYHEM (AND HERRING) (Book #6)

ADELE SHARP MYSTERY SERIES
LEFT TO DIE (Book #1)
LEFT TO RUN (Book #2)
LEFT TO HIDE (Book #3)
LEFT TO KILL (Book #4)
LEFT TO MURDER (Book #5)
LEFT TO ENVY (Book #6)
LEFT TO LAPSE (Book #7)
LEFT TO VANISH (Book #8)
LEFT TO HUNT (Book #9)
LEFT TO FEAR (Book #10)
LEFT TO PREY (Book #11)
LEFT TO LURE (Book #12)
LEFT TO CRAVE (Book #13)
LEFT TO LOATHE (Book #14)
LEFT TO HARM (Book #15)
LEFT TO RUIN (Book #16)

THE AU PAIR SERIES
ALMOST GONE (Book#1)
ALMOST LOST (Book #2)
ALMOST DEAD (Book #3)

ZOE PRIME MYSTERY SERIES
FACE OF DEATH (Book#1)
FACE OF MURDER (Book #2)
FACE OF FEAR (Book #3)
FACE OF MADNESS (Book #4)
FACE OF FURY (Book #5)
FACE OF DARKNESS (Book #6)

A JESSIE HUNT PSYCHOLOGICAL SUSPENSE SERIES
THE PERFECT WIFE (Book #1)
THE PERFECT BLOCK (Book #2)
THE PERFECT HOUSE (Book #3)
THE PERFECT SMILE (Book #4)
THE PERFECT LIE (Book #5)
THE PERFECT LOOK (Book #6)
THE PERFECT AFFAIR (Book #7)
THE PERFECT ALIBI (Book #8)
THE PERFECT NEIGHBOR (Book #9)
THE PERFECT DISGUISE (Book #10)
THE PERFECT SECRET (Book #11)
THE PERFECT FAÇADE (Book #12)
THE PERFECT IMPRESSION (Book #13)
THE PERFECT DECEIT (Book #14)
THE PERFECT MISTRESS (Book #15)
THE PERFECT IMAGE (Book #16)
THE PERFECT VEIL (Book #17)
THE PERFECT INDISCRETION (Book #18)
THE PERFECT RUMOR (Book #19)
THE PERFECT COUPLE (Book #20)
THE PERFECT MURDER (Book #21)
THE PERFECT HUSBAND (Book #22)
THE PERFECT SCANDAL (Book #23)
THE PERFECT MASK (Book #24)
THE PERFECT RUSE (Book #25)
THE PERFECT VENEER (Book #26)
THE PERFECT PEOPLE (Book #27)
THE PERFECT WITNESS (Book #28)
THE PERFECT APPEARANCE (Book #29)
THE PERFECT TRAP (Book #30)

THE PERFECT EXPRESSION (Book #31)
THE PERFECT ACCOMPLICE (Book #32)
THE PERFECT SHOW (Book #33)
THE PERFECT POISE (Book #34)
THE PERFECT CROWD (Book #35)

CHLOE FINE PSYCHOLOGICAL SUSPENSE SERIES

NEXT DOOR (Book #1)
A NEIGHBOR'S LIE (Book #2)
CUL DE SAC (Book #3)
SILENT NEIGHBOR (Book #4)
HOMECOMING (Book #5)
TINTED WINDOWS (Book #6)

KATE WISE MYSTERY SERIES

IF SHE KNEW (Book #1)
IF SHE SAW (Book #2)
IF SHE RAN (Book #3)
IF SHE HID (Book #4)
IF SHE FLED (Book #5)
IF SHE FEARED (Book #6)
IF SHE HEARD (Book #7)

THE MAKING OF RILEY PAIGE SERIES

WATCHING (Book #1)
WAITING (Book #2)
LURING (Book #3)
TAKING (Book #4)
STALKING (Book #5)
KILLING (Book #6)

RILEY PAIGE MYSTERY SERIES

ONCE GONE (Book #1)
ONCE TAKEN (Book #2)
ONCE CRAVED (Book #3)
ONCE LURED (Book #4)
ONCE HUNTED (Book #5)
ONCE PINED (Book #6)
ONCE FORSAKEN (Book #7)
ONCE COLD (Book #8)

ONCE STALKED (Book #9)
ONCE LOST (Book #10)
ONCE BURIED (Book #11)
ONCE BOUND (Book #12)
ONCE TRAPPED (Book #13)
ONCE DORMANT (Book #14)
ONCE SHUNNED (Book #15)
ONCE MISSED (Book #16)
ONCE CHOSEN (Book #17)

MACKENZIE WHITE MYSTERY SERIES
BEFORE HE KILLS (Book #1)
BEFORE HE SEES (Book #2)
BEFORE HE COVETS (Book #3)
BEFORE HE TAKES (Book #4)
BEFORE HE NEEDS (Book #5)
BEFORE HE FEELS (Book #6)
BEFORE HE SINS (Book #7)
BEFORE HE HUNTS (Book #8)
BEFORE HE PREYS (Book #9)
BEFORE HE LONGS (Book #10)
BEFORE HE LAPSES (Book #11)
BEFORE HE ENVIES (Book #12)
BEFORE HE STALKS (Book #13)
BEFORE HE HARMS (Book #14)

AVERY BLACK MYSTERY SERIES
CAUSE TO KILL (Book #1)
CAUSE TO RUN (Book #2)
CAUSE TO HIDE (Book #3)
CAUSE TO FEAR (Book #4)
CAUSE TO SAVE (Book #5)
CAUSE TO DREAD (Book #6)

KERI LOCKE MYSTERY SERIES
A TRACE OF DEATH (Book #1)
A TRACE OF MURDER (Book #2)
A TRACE OF VICE (Book #3)
A TRACE OF CRIME (Book #4)
A TRACE OF HOPE (Book #5)

Printed in Great Britain
by Amazon

42982040R00108